LITTLE RED
Wraith

LITTLE RED
Wraith

THE MIADIEN CHRONICLES
• VOLUME ONE •

LINDSAY
FLANAGAN

an imprint of
Roan & Weatherford Publishing Associates, LLC
Bentonville, Arkansas

Library of Congress Cataloging-in-Publication Data
Names: Flanagan, Lindsay author
Title: Little Red Wraith/Lindsay Flanagan
The Miadien Chronicles #1
Description: First Edition. | Bentonville: Mad Cat, 2024.
Identifiers: LCCN: 2024946243 | ISBN: 978-1-63373-984-0 (trade paperback) |
ISBN: 978-1-63373-985-7 (eBook)
Subjects: YOUNG ADULT FICTION/Fantasy/Epic |
YOUNG ADULT FICTION/Legends, Myths, Fables/General |
LC record available at: https://lccn.loc.gov/2024946243

Mad Cat paperback edition Ocotber, 2024

Cover & Interior Design by Casey W. Cowan
Map Illustration by K.M. Brown
Editing by Sabine Berlin, Amy Cowan & Lisa Lindsey

For Brooke,
my true North in a sky full of stars

ACKNOWLEDGMENTS

A massive amount of gratitude goes out to the people who read this manuscript in its earliest forms, when it was the sequel to *AnnaGrey and the Constellation* and not its own story and prequel to the AnnaGrey books. Thank you to Sabine Berlin, Devin Bradley, Tim Costello, and my editor and publisher, Amy Cowan, for seeing Anna's story as worthy to stand on its own. And also, thank you to Amy for being willing not only to publish this story, but two other companion books in the prequel series.

As always, thank you to my agent, Jessica Reino. I'm so grateful for your suggestion of writing an entire young adult companion series and championing my work. I'm so glad we're on a Laéth Realm journey together! Thank you also to Amy Brewer for representing my audiobook rights, and thank you to Tantor Audio for picking up my books.

I've been so lucky to rub shoulders with amazing authors at conventions, conferences, and other book events. Thanks (again) to Sabine Berlin for being my con buddy and to Cambria Williams for joining me at so many events. Booths are more fun with you two! Cambria, thanks for the pep talks to "just finish it!" because, hey, I finally did.

I had an incredible support group when the first volume of the

Laéth Realm Adventures came out. Lauri Schoenfeld and Melissa Dalton Martinez are the best PR people I know. James Owen and Monica Roe are two amazing authors who gave me incredible reviews and blurbs for *AnnaGrey and the Constellation*. So many family members and friends came to my first-ever book launch party, and I know I'll never be able to name you all, but if you were there, please know it meant more to me than all the stars in the sky. John, Nancy, Paula, and Ivanni, for putting together an amazing party at a beautiful venue with the best food. Dear Reader, go to Flanagan's on Main in Park City, Utah–you won't be sorry. (Last name is coincidental but definitely meant to be.)

I continue to be blessed with amazing beta readers and editors. Kortney Watkins, my "twin," who is always cheering me on and motivating me with encouragement and advice. Heather Harris-Bergevin and Evva Bergevin, for your continued support and professional feedback and suggestions for these books. Thank you to Korri Peterson for reading this draft and finding my typos! Kaylee Z., was my first non-family fan–the way you draw my characters is even better than what I envision in my mind. Adam V., thanks for being my authority on all things teenage-reader!

Angela Eschler and the EE team are the best co-workers an editor could ask for. My co-project managers run the entire show now, with minimal input from me so I can write my books. Huge thanks to Sandi for taking over my job, to Katrina for taking over other bits and pieces I can't keep up with, and to AJ for being willing to accept and roll with all the changes I've requested in the PM lineup. I've also been so lucky to have people want to intern for me, which is such an incredible honor. Thanks to Cambri Morris, Riley Bess, and Addison Gardner for sharing your time and talents with me.

My former college professors, Deb Thornton and Julie Nichols, for having me at UVU to talk to your students and teach about writing, publishing, and editing. I love that I get to continue being a Wolverine, even twenty years after graduating.

I'm so thankful to the other members of the team at Roan & Weatherford Publishing: Casey Cowan for the beautiful cover that stops people in their tracks, as well a fantastic overall design and layout; Lisa Lindsey for her super line editing skills; and K.M. Brown for the map of the Laéth Realm (which garners huge praise from everyone who sees it).

And finally, to my wonderful family, who I couldn't exist without. Mom and Brooke, thanks for our summer evening parties where we listen to old country and talk about the past so that it remains alive in us today. Beto, thanks for putting up with all the parties and also fixing my car all the time. Hannahlia, Rio, and Cayo, I love having you as my second set of kids. Carolyn, Austin, Shea, and Larissa, thanks for your love and support (and thanks to Austin and Shea for dogsitting!).

Dad, thanks for continuing to make me laugh, even though it's only in my memories now. I miss you.

Lily, thanks for being a fan of the books and discussing story lines and love triangles with me, and for being my art director on the maps and covers. Aislin, thank you for letting me read to you and for drawing the best pictures of my characters. Shawn, words can never express my appreciation to you for supporting me and this larger-than-life dream I have, for cheering me on, and for loving me despite all the time I spend on my laptop.

Finally, thank you to all the readers who have taken a chance on my stories. These characters couldn't exist without you opening the pages and reading them into life.

The Laéth Realm • *Map by K.M. Brown*

ONE

y sister always saw me even when no one else did. She never thought of me as less because I'm amorphous, unable to change into an animal form, never refused to claim me as her sister. But now she doesn't see me at all because she's lying under the cold ground.

Autumn leaves cleave to the edges of her headstone, but I let them lie where they fell, a bit of color on the gray, a bit of life even if dying. My fingers trace over my own name, etched there in honor. Anna's True North. My gaze lingers on the image of the wolf next to a dark-haired girl. My will hangs in a balance of dwelling in memories and living in the present. Between wanting to be seen or to be invisible since the only person who ever saw anything in me is gone.

I touch the wolf's image and wonder, as always, if I'd been able to change into my animal form and become incarnate, would I be a wolf like London or a fox like Mama? At fifteen, the last year a warsol body can change and integrate the changing bones and muscles, I'd lost my sister. Without her, I lost any desire to be who I could have been. Now I can't change.

The last rays of the day's dissolving sun shine on her name, one last light before the reign of night. They warm my face as I look to the west, expecting Papi's arrival from his errands in the village. He's a dark speck in the distance. I stand and shake the leaves from my skirt and push my wild red hair out of my eyes, then peer at the horse he's riding. It has an unfamiliar gait.

That's not Papi's horse.

His steed may have been wounded, which would mean he had to leave it in the village. I hope it didn't get hurt badly enough that it had to be put down. But the way this rider sits up straight in his saddle tells me that's not Papi, whose slightly curved back makes his shoulders hunch. I back away from the grave and sprint to the skeleton tree—the one London and I named because it's never had leaves, only limbs like bones— and huddle behind its enormous trunk.

I'm not expecting an attack, and I'm certainly no fighter. What can I do, an amorphous, against this incarnate soldier prowling on our land? The heavy branch that fell from this tree years ago, the one London and I called "Femur," lies near my feet in the thick grass where we always kept it, but I leave it where it rests. My best defense is to remain hidden.

The rider has gray hair, almost white, although he looks young, and his wide, silver eyes are big enough that they could be substituted for the moon. The pupils are round and full, unlike mine, which are half-moons.

He stops by the grave, blinking down at it for a moment, then clucks his horse forward again. I press my back against the skeleton tree and glance over my left shoulder, grimacing, and spin the ring I wear on my right hand, the one with the wolf head and fox head touching noses, as if I'm invoking some protection charm.

The rider's and horse's forms are silhouetted black against the now pink-and-purple sky. Stars open their eyes and wink down at us. The wild grass around the base of the skeleton tree is high enough that if I crouch low, it will mostly cover me, so I slide down the trunk and arrange the stalks around my body.

I'm so intent on making myself unseeable that I don't hear the footsteps until they are nearly on me.

Stifling a gasp, I hiss, "Redford!"

He jumps, but I catch his pant leg and pull on him, causing him to tumble down next to me.

"Hey! I didn't even see you!" Redford, London's fiancé, looks bemused.

He's not her fiancé anymore, of course. I've only seen him a handful of times since her funeral. According to rumor, he spends a lot of time in the pub. He grins as if we're playing a game like we used to, but the ache in his deep-set eyes is a tell that he still longs to be with London.

We have that in common.

"Why are you being so secretive?" he asks, not quietly.

"Shh! Look." I tilt my head toward the cottage where the strange warsol slinks around to the other side, out of view. And seemingly out of earshot, thankfully, because he doesn't come charging toward us at Redford's loudness.

Redford glances at where my house stands solid and undisturbed in the star-peppered dusk. Hoofbeats, slow and purposeful, come around the back of the cottage. The warsol appears in full view again, tall and fierce on his horse. Then, I see the emblem on his right shoulder. A phoenix, the sign of the queen.

"What is one of the queen's guards doing here? Alone?" Redford asks, blessedly whispering this time.

I flick my gaze across the pond to the heavily wooded hills. A whole company of the queen's soldiers could be lurking in there, waiting for a signal from the gray guard. But there is no reason for them to be. We live on the rim of Miadien, far from the queen's gaze.

The warsol sniffs, his wolfish nostrils flaring as if he's caught a scent on the edge of the breeze. I think it's *my* scent, even though Redford's is stronger. He smells like burning wood, a touch of grass, and a hint of ale.

The guard's lip curls. I duck lower, burrowing into the long field grass. Redford squats next to me, the length of his arm pressing against mine. The guard's silver eyes cut through the brush and lock onto us. He cocks his head.

"Oh, blackhole," Redford curses.

The gray guard climbs down from his horse, his movements slow and deliberate, and he sniffs, looking slightly perplexed, as if the scent isn't matching what he sees in the brush.

"Curse the red planets above," I mutter.

"Just stay down, London," Redford whispers.

My night vision allows me to see him perfectly, even though twilight has settled over us like a blanket. He blinks, and I flinch.

"I'm not London."

"No," he agrees, "you're not. You're Anna, and you shouldn't be hiding, afraid of everything. You should stand up and protect your home."

The ale may have given him the ability to smile earlier, but it doesn't take away the sorrow in the lines around his mouth and eyes. I think he sees the grief in mine, too. And the hurt.

TWO

edford doesn't apologize, but his eyes are soft when he looks down at me. Then, he stands, startling the incarnate.

"Oh," the guard says. "I was expecting a female based on the scent."

I struggle to get up in the thick grass. The guard looks slightly amused when he glances at me, but then he locks his gaze back on Redford. The two stare at each other, sizing the other up.

"Wolf." He nods at Redford.

"As are you," Redford replies.

I grind my jaw. Sometimes the incarnate are so obnoxious. This is one of the reasons I've told myself it's okay that I'm amorphous. It's bad enough when I compare myself to the other girls in the village in my human form—I don't need another skin to have to defend as valuable. The incarnate compare who changes into the smarter or stronger animal and, therefore, which is better. A wolf is brute force, but a fox is sly, and a coyote is cunning. But it's the wolves who always start the squabbling. Falling stars, the wolves. Arrogant dogs, all of them.

My sister was a wolf.

The guard turns so he's looking at me. He sniffs, a not-so-subtle reminder that he can smell me. "Thanks for saving me the energy of having to hunt for you."

"I didn't do it for you."

He lets out a beat of a laugh. One, like a gong, and it reverberates from my chest to my stomach. My knees buckle a little at his intense moonlight stare. He purposefully steps closer to me and away from Redford. My instinct is to back away, but Redford moves to stand solidly behind me, and London's ghost tells me to stay put. But ghosts aren't real, and Redford hasn't been here in such a long time, and who knows how long he'll stay without London. The guard raises his hand, the palm positioned right along my cheekbone as if he's going to slap me. I flinch, and Redford yelps, but he flicks his hand the other way and brushes a knuckle along my skin. My blood rushes, warming my skin.

"Red," the guard says, "like the dawn on the morning of a storm."

Redford's growl is barely audible, and the guard's horse nickers softly. Something brushes over the guard's eyes, like clouds over the moon. He breaks the contact, turning his profile to me, and says, "I'm looking for a woman. A fox named Belle."

He has a bruise on his cheek, shaped like the curved blade of a scythe. It wouldn't have been so noticeable had his skin not been as white as the glowing moon. He turns back to me, and I adjust my gaze.

"Belle is my mother," I say, my voice tight. "She's not here."

"Ah," he replies. "And who are you?" The corner of his mouth quirks up, so high his long, white canine tooth shows. His smile makes me think he somehow already knows my name.

"Anna."

"Greyson." He bows his head. "Will you give this letter to your mother?"

He hands me a thin envelope. I flip it over, finding it's

sealed with the phoenix. I whip up my head. "What does the queen want with my mother?"

"As to that, I can't tell you." He goes back to his horse and climbs on.

"Can't or won't?" Redford asks, but Greyson doesn't even acknowledge that he heard.

"What happened to your cheek?" I blurt. Now I've noticed it, it stands out like a burn scar on a mountain.

He flinches. "Training."

"The arnica plant can help," I say in a rush, wondering, even as the words spill out, why I want to help him.

"With what?" he asks. "Training?"

"The bruising."

He grins. "But then I'd fade my badge of honor."

I can't help smiling back.

"Are you training to be a healer?" he asks.

My heart sinks. It had been a dream once. But when there was nothing I could do to save my sister, I lost all faith in healing. I put away my herbs and oils and tried the bow and arrow, something she was talented at. I was horrible at it. I tried a sword, daggers, everything. I could no more save anyone with herbs now than I could have saved London from dying.

"I was," I say softly. "At one point."

"Do you have any?" Greyson asks. "Arnica, I mean."

"Just there. In the kitchen."

"How many coins is it?"

"I wasn't—it's nothing."

"Isn't it? Well. Thank you. I will take some."

I nod, glancing at Redford, whose expression is inscrutable, and rush into the kitchen to grab the last jar of arnica salve I had made. I peek out the window. Redford stands with his arms across his chest, glaring at Greyson, but Greyson seems unperturbed as he stares off at the horizon.

I come back out and hand Greyson the little jar. "You can apply it two to three times a day."

His fingers brush mine as he takes the salve. Our eyes meet, and I find that I don't want to look away. He gives me a small smile. "Thank you." His voice is soft, quiet, like a winter night when snow falls. But then he straightens in his saddle, and his soldier's mantle falls on him again. "By the way, I'd recommend you not hide from a queen's soldier again. They won't be as lenient on you as I was. When a queen's soldier comes to call, it's as if the queen herself is there. Mind that in the future, won't you?"

I swallow, wanting to retort that I don't give a wolf's droppings about the queen, who disdains all amorphous warsol as if we're lesser beings. Some of us choose not to change, but some of us can't change. Like me. And she thinks we're weak because of it.

"Oh," he says, almost lazily, "Redford. Expect to be drafted soon. If you were going to make any, uh, life-changing plans, I'd do them now." Greyson looks at me again, his gaze lingering just a touch too long. I could keep mine on him for a moon cycle, and looking away would be too soon. Abruptly, he turns his horse and gallops away.

"What a piece of—" Redford begins.

"Yes," I murmur, but I get the feeling my thoughts are not along the same lines as Redford's. "Wait a minute," I say, tearing my eyes away from the retreating horse and its rider. "How did he know your name, too?"

We look toward the gravestone. It sits alone, its outline stark and jagged, as if it's an errant puzzle piece of the sky. Redford's name is etched onto a fragment of it.

"But how did he know that's me?" Redford asks.

I think Greyson has been watching my family for quite some time.

THREE

edford and I go back to the cottage. My thoughts keep straying to the moonlit warsol, whose silver eyes bored into mine, whose touch made my heart pound in a way I'd only read about in stories. I don't know what compelled me to help him. He was a complete horse's arse. But he was also the first person who stirred my healer's heart, one I thought I'd buried with my sister.

But Redford feels like home to me, and I realize how homesick I have been for him. I could have gone to his cottage, which isn't even a mile away, but that would have meant facing the path without London. I should have, though, because his mother is expecting another child, and the pregnancy has made her ill. But I no longer gather any herbs that could help.

"Why did you—" he starts, but I know what he's going to ask, and I don't have any answers, so I cut him off.

"How's your mama?"

He pauses, but he doesn't push the issue. Instead, he says, "Still sick, but Clary came to help take care of her today, and Mama shooed me away."

"She's in good hands then," I say, thinking of the girl barely older than London who lives close to Redford. "Does she think the baby's a girl or a boy?"

"Mama said I never made her this sick—"

"Not until you were born."

He laughs and gives me a playful nudge. "So, she says it's probably a girl."

"A sister," I say, but my smile fades. I don't want to talk about sisters.

"Or the animal inside the baby isn't a wolf, like Mama." The ability to change into an animal form is another touchy subject for me but thankfully, Redford rushes on. "Either way, girl or boy, wolf or not-wolf, she wants to name the baby Rowan."

"Perfect name." I place the envelope Greyson gave me on the table where Mama can't miss it. My fingers itch to slice the seal and open the letter, but if there is one thing Mama demands, it's respect for her privacy.

"And your father?" I ask as I start a fire, hoping the smoke will alert Mama and she'll know it's time to come in. We were in the fields planting today, and she let me go home early after I had a crying spell when I found one of London's old earrings in the dirt. I'd thrown it back in the soil.

Dust to dust.

"He's okay. His heart seems to bother him more these days."

I stop bustling around the cottage for a moment, holding bread, fruit, and eggs unsteadily in my arms. "That fever.... Do you want dinner?"

Redford holds up a pan in response. It's nice having him here, having someone close to my age. Having someone whose heart is as broken as mine due to the loss of their best friend. I pray to the moon his father isn't lost to us soon, too. Waite was sick with a fever for weeks, which weakened his heart, slowed his body, and confused his mind. The fever happened right after they found out they were expecting the baby, and Redford confessed to Mama that his father likely wouldn't be around to take care of them.

"I heard some talk today," he says, diverting my thoughts, "at the quarry."

Our fathers work at the quarry to supplement their farm income, since the castle no longer buys food from the subjects. Queen Phoenix hired—enslaved, really, for the pittance she pays them—workers to farm food inside the castle walls. Well, Redford's father used to work there. Redford took his position after the fever, and my father helps them with their farm. Mama and I keep our farm going.

"What kind of talk? About being recruited?" I ask, frying eggs and glancing over my shoulder.

"No," Redford replies, his eyes not meeting mine. "Well, not exactly."

"What does that mean? And anyway, aren't you worried about being forced to join her ranks?"

"I will *not* be taken to her slaughter," Redford says, his voice harsh. The tone makes me cringe.

She won't slaughter you. *You're incarnate. Prized among warsol.*

"Phoenix will no longer sanction marriages between the amorphous and the incarnate."

I whip around. "That's—I mean—first of all, just because the amorphous choose not to change—or can't—doesn't mean we aren't warsol." But this isn't a new argument. It's not like we haven't said this before, demanded that the queen not treat us like second-class citizens. According to my father, Queen Phoenix's feelings regarding warsol who cannot change into their animal bodies were dormant after she took the throne from her father, as the warsol eased into life under a new sovereign. But apparently, those feelings were just napping because they are waking, and slowly, the amorphous are losing right after right.

And now, it seems she's going to govern who the incarnate can love.

"Why?" The question is simple. I want to add why does she care, why does it matter to her, as long as she has incarnate in her service. But Redford understands my unspoken questions, and he answers.

"No one actually said this, but the general consensus is she wants to breed out the amorphous from the incarnate lines."

I drop the pan of eggs onto the table and fold my arms. "So, she wants to make us disappear."

"She's supposed to sign the official declaration in the next couple of weeks or so."

"How can she even do that?"

Redford is on the other side of the room, away from the brightness of the fire. His eyes have lit up to a bright green. He blinks slowly, appearing almost feral in his anger. "She's the queen. She wants to make her race stronger."

"How does she plan on breeding out someone's choice to change or not?"

"It's assumed it will no longer be a choice."

I'm suddenly not hungry anymore, so I set the table only for three. I glance out the window, fuming. Mama is walking up the path from the fields. Papi hasn't returned yet, and I'm worried. I bite my lower lip and wrap my arms around my waist, trying to keep the anxiety from spilling out, trying to force some calm in.

"Then, what's to become of the amorphous?" I ask.

In Istreya, the neighboring kingdom ruled by the aeobanach and populated with their own kind and the paison they claim, their laws state only aeobanach can be joined in marriage to aeobanach, and only paison to paison. While aeobanach and paison are completely different races, we warsol are not—at least, I don't consider us two separate races—and Istreya is far away from us. Their laws regarding who can be wed and who is forbidden have never affected me. But now, I think more about it and wonder if a paison and an aeobanach have ever petitioned for a marriage, ever fought for that equal right.

"Truthfully?" Redford says. "The amorphous should show they are just as good as the incarnate, that their value isn't based on the shapes of their pupils or their ability to change into animals. They should let go of past hurts and use their supposed inabilities as abilities."

I raise my eyebrows. "Easy to say when you're incarnate."

"They should rise up. And the incarnate should recognize the value of their amorphous brothers and sisters."

"In a perfect place, maybe," I mutter.

"But there's something else, Anna," Redford says in a rush. "There's talk that Phoenix has selected an heir."

Phoenix has never married, nor has she ever had children. The closest thing she has to family is Skoll, the Crescent to the Crown, her distant cousin. His main duty involves keeping the crowes in check—keep Vermilliana, the self-titled princess of the crowes, from rebelling since Phoenix took over crowe lands.

"To protect them from the aeobanach," Phoenix had said. "We won't steal your tail feathers and force you to serve us." But she governs their lands so strictly that they belong to her just the same.

I look outside again. Mama is at the pump, washing the dirt off her hands.

Redford grabs my elbow and turns me to him. He puts both his hands on my shoulders and stoops to look into my eyes. I'm caught, not for the first time, by how beautiful his brown irises are, how the auburn in his beard reminds me of my own hair.

"Anna, before—before anything happens, before the proclamation or the oncoming war—because you know there will be one, the amorphous won't stand for this last blow. Or before I lose my nerve. Will you—" He bites his lip.

"What?" I ask.

"Marry me, Anna. I'll take care of you. Phoenix will never be able to get to us."

I stare at him. My first reaction is that I'm only sixteen, and my parents would never consent to my marrying so young. Agreeing to let London be engaged at sixteen was pushing it, and they had insisted she and Redford wait until they were eighteen to actually hold the ceremony. Not that marrying at sixteen is odd. Most warsol marry young and stay with their alphas for the rest of their lives, and their lives are not long when there is war. And there always seems to be a war, either boiling or simmering.

But apparently, Phoenix's law makes it necessary for me to marry now, or never marry at all. Unless I marry an amorphous, which isn't a bad thing, but to take away my choices of who I can and cannot marry is despicable. It's not like I've been going out into the village to meet someone, though. But before London died, anyone who ever took notice only recognized me as London's sister.

Mama comes in. Redford turns away from me and bows slightly to her.

I go to the table and slice the bread. "Evening, Mama," I say in a tight voice, hoping she doesn't notice the flush on my skin.

"Hello, love. Are you doing better?" She doesn't wait for me to respond but speaks to Redford. "Redford, always a pleasure. How's Delilah? And the growing pup? I can't wait to get my hands on him or her."

Redford gives Mama a peck on the cheek. "I'm sure my mama would be glad for a visit from you."

"Your father isn't back yet," Mama says to me, not questioning, but stating. Worry is drawn into the lines around her mouth, across her forehead. She gives me a quick squeeze, smelling of dirt and rosewater, feeling like safety and home.

"No," I reply. "And a soldier came and brought you a letter." I point at it with the bread knife.

Her gaze follows the point of my knife and lands on the phoenix seal. Mama's face drains of color. She snatches the letter off the table and rips it open, turning her back to us, her shoulders hunched near her ears. Redford and I exchange glances. When Mama faces us again, the color has returned to her face, but I notice her fox-ears have started to elongate.

She silently hands the letter to me. It's written in spidery black ink.

> *Come and meet with me, Belle of the Foxes. It's been far too long. Linden is my honored guest and will stay here and visit with me until you come and fetch him. This letter will allow you passage. Enter at the south gates.*
>
> *Your ever-loving and faithful friend,*
> *Phoenix*

Questions as numerous as the stars flash at me, but the first one to pop out is, "Since when do you and the queen know each other personally?"

Mama's lips press so tightly together they are white instead of their usual maroon. "I shouldn't have let him go," she says rather than answering me.

But Papi had gone to the village, not to the capital. And why shouldn't he have gone? He goes all the time, alone or with Mama, and there has never been any trouble other than a few comments from incarnate about Papi being a "useless amorphous." But we're so used to it that we just wad up their insults like paper and throw them into the smoldering coals of our anger, kindling for what we will do when we can no longer stand it.

Was Phoenix in the village? What would the queen have been doing here? She wouldn't have come without fanfare, without a billion guards, without—

Guards. *Greyson.*

Had he been part of the group who had taken Papi? Had Greyson helped pull Papi from his horse, knock him in the head, bound him—

My over-anxious imagination runs away from me, as it always does. I don't have any evidence that what happened to Papi was violent. But Papi wouldn't have gone willingly, or at least not without sending us a message.

Unless he knew Phoenix had ordered Greyson to bring us the letter.

"Redford," Mama says, drawing me out of my thoughts, for which I am grateful because they might spin off into another worst-case scenario, "may I ask you to take Anna with you to your home and watch over her while I'm gone?"

"Of course," Redford says.

"I will leave at first light."

"But could I convince you to allow me to escort you? Anna can stay with my mama and papi, and Clary is there, too, taking care of my mother. Anna would be safe with Clary, who is a good fighter as well as healer. If Queen Phoenix has taken Linden against his will, the road might be dangerous for you, and—"

"It won't be unsafe for me," Mama says. She holds up the letter as if we need a reminder that in a twisted way, the queen has invited Mama to the capital.

"You understand I wouldn't have been able to live with myself if I didn't offer."

Mama smiles warmly at him. "I know, and I appreciate it, my dear. You are the best of young men." She retrieves some blankets and pillows and places them on the rug by the fire. "You can sleep in your old bed."

They both smile, lips curved upward but trembling slightly. How can they tolerate the bittersweet?

"Thank you again for offering," Mama continues, "but I would appreciate your protection of my daughter more."

Redford bows his head, and she leans in and kisses him on top of his brown locks. He won't push her anymore, but London would have. London wouldn't have let her go alone, but I will, as usual, stand by and let the dice land where they will.

FOUR

he coals have died down to mere sparks, and Mama, Redford, and I have been sitting up late, sipping whiskey and talking of old times, touching briefly on London, but mostly focusing on things we'd done as a group—Redford's family and ours. From lake-swimming outings to late-night firelight chats like this one, when Waite's health was better, Papi wasn't held captive, and London was alive.

Redford's grin is bigger now, his eyes sparkling like amber gems in the firelight, switching to pretty peridot jewels when he leans away from the light. Mama's lips have returned to their brilliant maroon, the color that made every other woman in the village jealous because she doesn't have to use lip stain. My hair probably stands on end because I run my fingers through it with every drink I take.

If London was here, she would already be halfway to the castle to demand Papi's return. If London was here, she would force me to grow a spine and do something. If London was here… but she is *not* here.

There is only me.

"Well, my darlings," Mama says, using the term of endearment she once used for London and me, "I must get to bed, as do you. We have an early start—"

"Yes," I say, "we do. I'm going with you." The words surprise even me.

Redford draws in a breath.

Mama glances between Redford and me, and I swear I hear her thoughts. *Anna is the complacent one who does what she's told. She never argues, just goes along with the plans....*

"Anna—"

"Mama. The queen has captured my father and requested your presence. I can't lose any more of my family."

"That will not happen. Papi and I will be back soon. I refuse to take you to her court," Mama says, her tone sharp and on point like an axe.

"What, is she going to demand that you trade me for Papi? She wouldn't want me. I'm worth less to her than Papi because at least he—" I cut myself off. *At least he gets out and does things,* I'd almost said. "London would have gone," I say instead, "and you would have let her."

You aren't London. Redford's words from earlier practically scream in my brain.

No, I'm not. But I'm the only daughter Mama and Papi have left, so I will do what she would have done and be the daughter they lost.

Mama stares at me, long and hard. The coals crackle in the background, and an owl hoots outside.

"I'll escort you," Redford says softly. "We can stop by my place to let my mama know, and I'll take you both there."

"Your mother is due to give birth soon," Mama says.

"I will ask Clary to stay. I can't let you go alone."

Mama turns her stern gaze on him now. Her shoulders relax when she looks at him, and her eyebrows straighten out of their V-formation. "I don't believe I need the protection."

They both glance at me, then Redford nods. "But you don't know what you're getting into."

Mama sighs and runs her fingers through her long, dark hair, so much like London's, except Mama's is threaded with silver, little interruptions in an otherwise black waterfall, and it spills disheveled over her shoulders. "Oh, but I think I do," she says, but it's low, not meant for us, despite our ability to hear sounds better than aeobanach, paison, and crowes combined. "That's kind of you, Redford. You may escort us there, but then I want you to come right back. When we have Linden, we will have additional protection."

"Understood," Redford replies.

Mama leaves, heading to her room, and she shuts the door behind her. Redford's gaze is on me, but I keep my eyes pointed to the dying firelight. It's not lost on me that Mama didn't actually give me permission or agree to my request. She acquiesced to Redford, knowing he would take care of me so she didn't have to.

Redford touches my hand, brushing my fingertips with his. I shift my gaze from the embers and give him a brief smile, letting him know I appreciate his help.

"Anna, about before—what I asked you when your mother came in—"

"You're taking it back?"

"No, of course not. I just wondered if—if you'd considered it, is all."

"I considered it, but I need time." I can't make any decisions right now. I have too much on my mind regarding my father—seemingly a guest of the queen's but more likely her prisoner—and how my mother is on an apparent first-name basis with the queen.

He asked me to marry him, but was it out of duty? Duty to his promise to keep me safe, to my family because he was once meant to be part of us, and to an oath he already swore to my sister. An oath that I'm now to take in her stead, like a shadow waiting in the wings. Another role I will fulfill in my sister's place.

FIVE

The next morning dawns red, the clouds of an oncoming thunderstorm lounging on the mountains in the distance. It's as if the storm is waiting for travelers to be out in the unprotected open before climbing down from its perch and letting loose.

I pull my cloak tighter, shivering. If I could turn incarnate, I could don my fur coat and warm myself. But I have tried to change. Every year since I was twelve, I kept waiting for the moment when I could. But although I have the warsol fangs, I have no animal inside me, or if I do, it's dormant.

We arrive at Redford's home right as the clouds pick themselves up and start marching to meet us. We get inside his family's little cottage as the sky breaks open.

"Redford!" Delilah rushes as quickly as she can in her enlarged state and hugs her son. "I assumed you stayed the night because you were having too much fun reuniting with Anna." She smiles and limps toward me. As she moves, her skirt lifts, revealing how swollen her ankles are. We hug, and I kiss her cheek. She looks miserable, but she has a brightness in her eyes that seems to dim everything else.

"And Belle," Delilah says, moving to Mama. I know Delilah loved London like a surrogate daughter and was almost as heartbroken as my parents when she died. And then she became pregnant with this miracle child—after Redford, they had never been able to have more children, and, all these years later, another pup is finally joining their family—but then Waite fell so sick.

Tragedies and miracles.

Plagued and blessed.

"You remember Clary?" Delilah says, indicating to the young woman who stirs something over the cook fire. "She's training to be a midwife and healer and decided I was her practice patient." Delilah laughs, as does Mama.

Clary grins, her blonde curls getting frizzier the longer she stands by the steaming pot.

"Yes," both Mama and I say. Mama does the nice thing and asks after her health and her family's, but a twinge of jealousy pierces my heart. I knew Clary was interested in healing like I was, but it seems she pursued her dream, while I effectively killed mine.

"Clary," Redford says as he helps Delilah sit, "I have a favor to ask of you. I'll pay you what I can, but I need someone to stay here with Mama while I escort Anna and Belle to the castle."

"Why are you going to the castle?" Delilah interrupts.

Mama withdraws the envelope from her cloak pocket and hands it to Delilah.

She reads the letter, mouthing the words as she skims the contents. She pales. "Oh, Belle."

Clary comes over, wiping her hands on her apron. "Of course. No need to pay me other than in room and board. Is everything all right?"

Mama and Delilah exchange a look, one I don't understand. Mama says, "Yes, everything is fine. I just have a transaction to conduct at the castle."

Clary's raised eyebrows indicate she knows Mama is lying,

but I can also tell she knows it's none of her business because she turns back to the stove and says, "We were just about to have breakfast. Can I pack you some to take on the road?"

I smile gratefully at Clary and decide it's not her fault I gave up on healing. "That would be great," I say, moving to help her. "Where are you doing your training?"

"I spent the last six months with Amethyst," Clary says, blushing slightly, and it's no wonder. Amethyst is the lead castle healer and mother to Skoll, the Crescent, who is a healer as well as a soldier. She doesn't take just any apprentice.

"Wow, Clary," I say, unrolling cheesecloths for her to pack food in. "I didn't know that."

"Well, you have been—" She pauses, and I know what she's going to say. Hiding. Buried like London, except mine has been in grief instead of in the ground. After a quick glance at me, Clary pushes forward with the small talk rather than commenting on my prolonged mourning. "I apprenticed with the village healer for a year, and he believed I was skilled enough to get further education, so I went to the castle to compete for a spot at Amethyst's month-long training. The top five got to further compete for a spot, and I.... Well." She blushes again as we pour hot coffee into traveling mugs.

"Then I know why Redford has no qualms about leaving his mother—and his father—with you."

Her gaze flicks to the door at the back of the room, where I assume Waite rests. "I wish I could do something more for him, but perhaps when I go back to Amethyst, I can ask her what she thinks."

"When do you go back?"

"I... I think I might be, well, ordered to return."

It's like a knife in the back. "You'd heal incarnate soldiers."

"I would do my job to repay the castle for my training," Clary says quickly. "You know I don't believe—"

"I understand," I say shortly.

"Anna," she says, grabbing my arm. I want to wrench it

away, but her pale blue eyes snag my gaze as if they have hooks. "After you take care of whatever you need to at the castle, you should go to Adderin. Or even Istreya. I wouldn't want anything to happen to you."

"Heard talk in the castle, have you?" I ask, still unable to move my gaze away from her penetrating stare.

"A bit. And you should know Skoll's heart—"

I raise my eyebrows. The flush on her cheeks is back, but this time I don't think it has anything to do with her being humble. She releases her fingers from my arm, leaving red half-moons in my skin.

"I'm sorry," she says.

"I get what you're saying." I rub my arm, trying to erase the marks. It doesn't hurt, but the shape of the imprints remind me of my eyes, the ones that identify me as amorphous. "Thank you for the food. And for taking care of Delilah and Waite."

"Of course. You were once interested in becoming a healer, weren't you?"

"Things change," I say quietly, and Clary gives me a sympathetic look.

"Clary," Redford says, "can we talk for a moment before I leave?"

Clary leaves me to finish wrapping the food. I assume they are going to talk about what type of care his parents need, but they step outside where they can't be overheard.

When they come back in, Mama says, "Are we ready?" Her tone indicates she is impatient to go.

"Yes, Mama." I give Delilah a quick kiss on the cheek and her belly a small pat. "Take care of your mama, little Rowan."

Redford takes longer to say goodbye to Delilah, so Mama and I give them privacy and go to the horses. The rain has stopped, but it's wet and cold. I grab an extra cloak from my pack, and we're mounted and ready when he comes out. He's tucking something small into the pocket of his coat. It glints gold, the cloud-covered morning making it seem brighter.

I have a guess as to what it is. London's engagement ring. The one he took from her still finger. I wonder if he always carries it with him, or if he just now retrieved it from his room.

Either way, we both carry a piece of my sister with us. He probably thinks it brings him safety and luck.

But mine, the wolf-and-fox ring, haunts me.

SIX

I t had been an accident. London always rode the most spirited horses, the ones that were the most difficult to break and train. She'd been trying to break Lassiter, her colt, for months. Redford once suggested getting help from the aeobanach, but she'd scoffed and instead taken the black horse every day to the woods to run. She said she'd break that horse if it killed her.

In the end, it did.

On her final day, she'd taken Lassiter on a ride after seeing me off to school. The last image I have of her is of Lassiter racing across the green land under a dark, thundercloud sky, London's dark hair flying behind her like a banner.

My father and Redford brought home her limp body. I tried every herb in my limited arsenal, but I knew it was already too late. Nothing could bring back the dead. Papi let Lassiter run wild in the woods. I've never seen him again. We buried London, and nothing has been the same since. I quit school and kept vigil at her grave for days until Papi finally put his foot down and told me he didn't want two dead daughters. I needed to start living again.

The first night I wasn't at her graveside, we woke to find the dirt disturbed and the headstone tilted on its side. We speculated about what it could have been. A warsol pack in animal form, playing around or fighting, not paying attention to where they were running. Or perhaps a runaway horse—maybe even Lassiter. It never happened again, and we never spoke of it again, either.

Redford rides next to me, his knee bumping against mine, shaking me out of my nightmares. He hasn't asked about marriage again, but he hasn't forgotten. He keeps looking at me, and I know he's watching for any sign of an answer. But he doesn't push me, and I appreciate that.

He also looks like he wants to say something, and I wonder if it has to do with his conversation with Clary. He stepped outside for it, so I assume he was hiding whatever he had to say from me, or maybe his mother.

The rain has started again in thick, dark sheets, making the road in front of us barely visible. The horses push against the storm, and Berne, my roan gelding, stumbles in the soup-like mud on the road. Mama and Redford have suspended themselves between animal and human, donning their fur coats. Mama, a black fox, is beautiful in the gray day, the wind whipping her black hair, the maroon of her lips the only color present. I always thought it looked strange when the incarnate suspended themselves between animal and human, but it is certainly easier—so I've been told—to ride a horse in only part-animal form than in full-animal form. Many incarnate ride this way, suspended between the two forms, rather than running on their own four animal legs. Some simply enjoy riding, like London. Others ride to save their energy.

I think it's fitting that the weather is dark, cold, and foreboding because that's what our destination is, too. I wish I could talk to someone. No, not just someone. My sister. My other half. We shared blood, parents, histories. Secrets. Dreams.

The horses struggle in the thick mud, and I am soaked to

the bone. On a good day, the trek to the castle only takes ten to twelve hours. But in this mess, it's taking much longer. Mama and Redford, if they didn't have me as a burden, could change into their animal forms and run the rest of the way, not having to deal with the horses. But they do have me.

The Lamplight Inn is a blessed mile away, and when we stop there, I sigh with happiness. I slide off my horse, giving him a quick pat as Redford takes the reins and leads him, along with the other two mounts, to the stables, while Mama and I go inside. She talks to the innkeeper about food and a room for the night. Shivering, I move to the fireplace and pull off my cloak, hanging it on a rack full of other travelers' wet things.

"Looks like you could use some dry clothes," a voice to my right says.

I nearly buckle at the knees. Greyson, standing near the window, his gray hair looking silver in the firelight, grins at me.

"I bet you wouldn't think I'd have ladies' clothing on hand, but luckily for you, I do," he says as he moves closer.

I eye him, noticing his bruise has faded considerably. "Why would you have ladies' clothing? You take them as tokens from all your conquests?" I wave my hand at him. "I don't need help from the queen's lapdog."

Greyson chuckles. "No, not from my conquests. Would it surprise you to know I deliver clothing to those in need?"

I look for a hint of jest in his sparkling gray eyes.

He holds up his hands as if in surrender. "Shocking, I know. But someone has to do it."

"The queen—" I begin, but Greyson shakes his head, almost imperceptibly.

"Just me. And my brother."

"Is he a lapdog, too?"

Greyson's smile fades. "No. I wouldn't allow it." He goes back to the window and pulls on a cloak, then nods to me and slips out into the storm.

Bewildered, I turn back to the fire, wishing I'd taken him

up on his offer of dry clothes, berating myself for not drilling him about my father, and wondering why he won't allow his brother to serve the queen.

Redford comes in a moment later, shaking water from his fur as he changes into a full human again. He smiles at me, and I return it, warmed by his brown eyes that remind me of chocolate. His hair looks even more red in the firelight, like autumn leaves clinging to their color before they give in to brown. His face is so familiar, so much like home.

He comes to the fire and holds his hands out to warm them. "Where's your mama?"

I scan the room, then spy the table where Mama has settled. She's speaking to the server, and my stomach growls at the thought of food. I gesture with my head to where she sits.

"There's something I wanted to tell you. It wasn't a coincidence that I was near your home the other night." Redford pauses, and I lean in, waiting for him to continue. "I was on a mission. For the amorphous—"

The door of the inn opens again, and a rush of cold air skitters across my back. The shiver that quakes me must be more violent than I think because it is what caused Redford to break off as he reaches out to steady me.

"You're cold," he says at nearly the same moment Mama gestures for us to join her at the table. Looking as if he was caught like a thief, Redford goes toward Mama but glances back at me with questioning eyes.

"In a moment," I say, "after I warm up."

I wonder if he can sense my lie. The shiver didn't come from the autumn air or the fact that my clothes are still damp. It's because the gray soldier is near.

As soon as Redford walks away, Greyson steps close. "I wonder, Anna, if you'll ever find another true North."

Holding my breath, I slowly face him. He doesn't blink or smile, but simply places a bundle in my arms. It's warm and dry, and I hug it to my chest. His eyes are like wintery moons.

"What do you want from me?" It's not what I had intended to say, but it spills from my mouth like uncorked wine.

He shakes his head. "I don't want anything *from* you."

His implication makes me grow hot even though I'm not yet dry. "Why? I'm amorphous, and your queen is about to outlaw incarnate warsol from ever marrying an amorphous."

Greyson sighs as he runs one hand through his smoky hair. "It's been the cause of a lot of the unrest in the villages outside the castle. I didn't know the rumors had reached this far."

"Rumors? Or fact?"

He shakes his head. "I won't know until she signs. And she's your queen, too, Anna. Be careful what you say. You could be branded a rebel."

"Do you have a hot iron nearby?" It's something London would have said, and the reaction Greyson gives me is what I wanted—the look of surprise, then the serious, intent stare.

The flames from the fire reflected in those eyes look like molten metal. "Careful, Anna," he says again, turning to leave, but I catch him by his sleeve.

"Was it you?"

He wrinkles his brow.

"My father. He didn't go to the castle. He went to the village, and the queen was just conveniently there?"

"The queen was not in your village. I don't—"

"The letter was from the queen."

"I know." He tries to grin, but it slides from his lips before it is fully formed.

"Anna?" Redford interrupts us right when I was going to get—*hoping* to get—answers. I grit my teeth.

Greyson takes a step back and nods at Redford. "I'm just giving Anna some dry clothes," he explains. "She looks awfully cold, don't you think?"

Redford barely tilts his chin at Greyson. "Anna, the food is here." He holds out his arm, but I don't take it.

"I'll be right there."

Redford drops his hand but once again leaves me alone by the fire and returns to Mama, who's watching me.

I turn back to Greyson, knowing I have to be quick. "We're on our way to the castle. Phoenix has my father. Do you know anything about that?"

"I don't know much, but I know he's not hurt."

"Why aren't you already back at the castle?"

"I took a detour to my home. Checked in on my mother and brother."

"They live around here?"

"To the east. I had another errand to do on my way back."

"What was that?"

Greyson smiles. "Most people hope to outrun a storm, Anna of the Foxes, when the morning breaks red. But I hoped to be right in the middle of it. Thank you, by the way, for the arnica. I look much better now, don't I?"

SEVEN

'm glad I have the excuse of being too close to the fire to explain my flushed face. Greyson leaves with a swish of his gray cloak, and I stumble to the table where Mama and Redford wait.

Mama eyes me like a fox after prey.

"He's the soldier who delivered the letter, and I asked him questions about Papi."

Mama is halfway out of her seat as if to chase Greyson down, but I hold up my hand. "It's no use. He doesn't know anything."

"Or he's not telling us anything," Redford growls. "Why would he?"

He already has an empty mug next to him. One pint of ale down, how many more to go? I don't reply. What would I say? It's true. Greyson has no reason to be truthful with me. His queen is my enemy, and he is her watchdog. He practically admitted it.

"What did he give you?" Mama says, gaze fixed on the bundle I'm still holding tightly to my chest.

"Clothes," I reply.

Mama raises her eyebrows, and Redford scowls.

"He knows you're amorphous," Mama says.

"How could he not?" I reply, an edge to my tone. "I'm sopping wet, so obviously I didn't have a fur coat protecting me. And he's also seen my eyes."

"You let him get too close to you," Redford says.

I turn my head slowly to him. He's halfway through his second mug, but I don't care if he's starting to feel numb. When he and London would have small arguments, she would always win. He'd back down as soon as she gave him a certain look. I stare at him, wondering if he sees the ghost of her in my features until he looks away. To his credit, he looks abashed.

"Sorry," he mutters.

Mama looks between us, then says, "The food will stay warm. Go change into the dry things. The moon above knows I don't need you getting sick on the road."

I can hear what she's not saying. The moon knows I shouldn't be on the road with her.

"Upstairs, third room on the right," Mama says.

My chair scrapes against the wooden floor as I push back from the table and leave without another word. I find the room easily, and the door shuts with a quiet click. I breathe in, calming my simmering anger and frustration, and blink a few times, willing myself not to shed tears. The moon above—she's rather wise—knows I've cried far too many times this past year.

I lay out the clothes on the bed. They look handmade but are intricately sewn. The black tunic and coat are made from soft, sleek cotton, the riding pants are a black leather, and the cloak, deep red, has been spun from thick wool. The gloves, also wool, are black. Smiling, I run my fingers over the softness of them, and though they are beautiful, I find myself wishing they were gray. It hasn't escaped my notice that it has become my favorite color, that I seek the hue in every place I turn. There's also a small bouquet of dried chamomile and a bag of mixed herbs that smell of pine and cranberries. The fresh, clean scent reminds me of the winter solstice festival. Chamomile is easy enough to come by, and it's also pretty. The pine and cranberries look lovely in the little bag he gave me, too, but the mixture isn't anything I've seen before, and cranberries aren't easy to find.

I can't fathom why he would give me such a beautiful gift. It can't be just because of the arnica. I don't think the queen's soldiers even feel guilt. Moreover, why would he care about an amorphous like me? And why in the starriest skies above would he have clothing and herbs that seem to be made just for me?

I sit next to the clothes on the large bed, which takes up most of the space in the room. A wash basin behind a dressing screen sits in the corner, and a lush rug covers the floor. I guess I know where Redford will be sleeping. My wet clothes are making my skin itch, so I peel them off and hang them on the line strung near the fireplace. I relish the softness of the tunic as it slides over my shoulders and arms, the way the pants hug my legs, the smell of the pine lingering on the cloak.

Curling up on the rug in front of the flickering fire and drifting off to sleep sounds more enticing than food with Mama and Redford's accusing eyes and questions, but my stomach argues with me, so I leave the comfort of my momentary solitude and go back downstairs, marveling at the way the cut of the coat fits my waist perfectly, wondering how he found the perfect clothes for my body.

Mama and Redford both eye me as I sit down, but I avoid their gazes. We eat in silence, punctuated intermittently by the conversations of others. I want to talk to Mama about something, but it's not for the ears of nosy warsol.

When we're finished, Redford goes to the fireplace and engages in a conversation with some of the inn's guests. It seems like he knows one of them because they break off from the group and go to the corner of the room. The man's hair is so blond it's almost white, and his eyes glow not from his night vision but because they, too, are white. The conversation seems

heated, with hand gestures, reddened faces, and veins and ten-
dons popping out of necks.

"Who is that?" I ask Mama, nodding to the man Redford
speaks with.

"I don't know. Maybe someone from the quarry?"

I don't think so. What could have happened at the quarry
that would cause that vehement of an interaction?

Mama and I go to the room, and I am loathe to take off my
clothes again and trade them for a nightdress. But I'm filthy
from the rain, so Mama calls for hot water to be brought up,
and I bathe behind the screen, letting the heat dissolve into
my skin, loosening my muscles. I think about Redford and
hope he's all right. The man he argued with looked angrier
than Redford.

But I'm also thinking about Mama and Phoenix.

"Mama?" I call.

"Yes, love?"

"I need to know why."

Mama is quiet, but her soft footsteps tell me she's pacing.
"Why Phoenix has your father?"

I don't reply. Obviously, that's what I want to know. Papi
hasn't done a thing against the crown—except be amorphous—
and we live so far from the castle, close to the Adderin border,
and only go to the village when necessary. It doesn't make sense
that the queen would capture Papi.

"You know I was born in the capital city," Mama begins. I
stop swishing the water so I can hear her clearly. "My father was
a close friend and advisor to the then-king, Phoenix's father."

I knew my grandfather had served the crown, but Mama
never talked much about it, and the fact isn't that odd. Most
warsol who live in the capital serve the monarch in one way or
another. Mama had always just said she never fit in, and Papi
had provided her a way out. London and I never questioned it.
We were happy, and there was no reason to wander back to the
capital because our grandparents were long dead.

"My father brought me to the castle with him often," Mama said. "Phoenix and I were playmates."

This is new information. I sit up straighter in the tub, leaning toward the screen. My mother was a childhood friend of the princess? Then again, I'm sure Princess Phoenix was as rotten as Queen Phoenix and went through friends like she does underwear.

"We even trained together as soldiers in our teens."

I always knew Mama was good with a sword and could defend herself. She was even better with a bow and arrow, like London. The skills she taught my sister—and tried to teach me—must be the same ones she'd learned by the evil queen's side.

I pull myself out of the water and dry off.

"But the same thing happened to Phoenix and me that happened to our fathers. They had a falling out because my father disagreed with some of the king's methods. I eventually came to disagree with her ideas and practices as well."

I poke my head around the screen as I put on a nightdress.

Mama looks over at me. "I've tried to remain as far away from her as possible. I don't want her in my life."

I come out from behind the screen and sit next to Mama. "Well, she obviously wants you in hers."

"Apparently. She found me."

I raise my eyebrows. "You were hiding?"

"I was doing my best to stay unnoticed."

"Why did you stay in Miadien, then?"

"It's home," Mama says simply.

"So, the queen taking Papi. You think she wants you to be some sort of advisor to her?"

Mama snorts. "No. She knows I'd advise her to let the amorphous have the same rights as the incarnate. I'd advise her against deceiving the crowes. She'd throw me out flat on my backside like she did all those years ago."

I chuckle softly at the image that flashes through my head—

Mama being tossed unceremoniously from the castle and landing on her arse.

Smiling, Mama ruffles my hair. "Climb into bed. We'll find out soon enough what Phoenix wants."

EIGHT

By early afternoon, the sun has dried the land, and we've reached the outlying villages of the castle. Evidence of the recent unrest Greyson mentioned litters the area we ride through. Homes smolder from fires, wagons are upturned, and soldiers patrol the streets. I burrow deeper in my cloak, hoping no one will notice my half-moon eyes. But in this chill, most of the incarnate are sporting their fur coats for protection, so I stand out anyway.

"Redford," I ask as we ride, "who was the man you were talking with at the inn? He seemed upset."

Redford flicks his gaze to Mama's back. "Just someone from the quarry."

A lie. He doesn't want Mama to know who he was talking to.

"Oh. Well, I'm glad you got it figured…." Nothing I say will make sense. I wonder if he'll tell me when Mama isn't around, and that makes me even more curious. He did, I recall, try to talk to me at the fireplace. But that was before his argument, so I'm not sure if what he was going to say has anything to do with the man.

We stop for lunch, a picnic of food we'd packed from the

inn, and sit on drying stumps while the horses graze. I don't know if Mama told Redford about her past relationship with Phoenix, and he and I haven't had a moment alone, so I haven't been able to tell him. But whether he knows or is going into the castle blind with us, the fact that he's here, that he's loyal to us, makes me warm inside, as if I've just taken the first sip of morning coffee.

I realize with a start that I love Redford. I've always loved him. But I don't know if it's enough. I know for certain that while it's warm and comforting, it's not sharp and exhilarating, like what I have felt for Greyson since the moment he came around my cottage on his horse.

Redford takes the horses to a creek for water, while Mama and I clean up. He comes back, and we mount quickly so we can continue our journey. By late afternoon, the spires of the black castle appear. Mama leads us to the south gates as if she's traveled this path dozens of times. She probably has, although it was years ago. I wonder what has changed since the last time she was here. The guards standing sentry hold up their hands to halt us, and Mama procures the envelope from her pocket and passes it to one of the guards. He peers at the seal, then flips it open and reads the letter. Nodding to the other guard, he gives it back to Mama, and just like that, we're admitted into the royal compound.

Its onyx stone walls rise above us, topped with battlements that look like slashes against the purple sky. Blue lights begin to appear in windows now that dusk is settling over us, the flames licking the stones like tongues licking teeth. Mama shows the letter to two other sets of guards before we're finally shown to the stables, where a stable hand takes our horses. Curiously, he's a paison. His russet skin, orange feathers, and red plume offer much-needed color in this dark place.

I have kept my hood up, and I don't lower it once we're inside the walls. A soldier—yet another person who needs to check the letter—escorts us down several cold corridors. Blue flames flicker in sconces shaped like wolf, fox, and coyote heads in an alternating pattern that line the hallway. I want to glance behind me at Redford, but his boots make soft steps on the hard floor, proof he's there, so I remain face-forward. We finally stop at a large antechamber rather than in a throne room, where I expected we'd be taken.

"Wait here," the soldier says.

There are no chairs, so we stand on the stone floors, waiting. I spin my wolf-and-fox ring and try not to grind my teeth. Redford shuffles his feet. Mama's face is set like stone, but her fists are clenched, and her jaw is tight. A vein flickers in the center of her forehead, a telltale sign of barely controlled rage.

A door on the left opens, and Greyson strides in. *Blackhole.* He doesn't meet my stare, instead fixing his gaze on a spot above our heads. I'm half-tempted to look up and see what has captured his attention, but he holds out his right hand and says, "Her Majesty, Queen Phoenix of Miadien, awaits you." He gestures for us to enter the room.

I've never seen the queen in person before, but the drawings and paintings of her have been fairly accurate. She is resplendent in a scarlet gown and black cloak. Her hair, red as an eclipsed moon, is pulled back into a bun, and a braid crowns her head. She wears no other diadem. She's draped in her throne as if she's part of it and looks at us as if we're casual visitors, not the family of a man she's captured.

Mama gives a short bow, and Redford and I follow suit, although it hurts my pride and my knees to bend to her.

"Belle," Phoenix croons, "it's been a long time. Too long, don't you agree?"

"I'm on the opposite spectrum, Phoenix, thinking it's not been long enough."

The queen cackles. "You haven't changed, Belle."

"Neither have you, Phoenix. Where is my husband?"

"Straight to the point. Greyson?"

Greyson opens the door, and guards lead Papi in, unchained

and unhurt. Mama lets out a breath of relief, but my head is light, and the room has a slight blur to it. I can't let myself appear weak in front of the queen. Staring at Papi, I search his face, his arms, everything I can, for a sign of injury. He gives me a watery smile, and even though he's not physically hurt, I know something is wrong.

"You've been hard to locate all these years, Belle," Phoenix says. I draw my attention away from my father and back to the queen. "I was surprised to find you still in Miadien."

"Miadien is my home," Mama returns with a snarl.

Phoenix raises one red eyebrow. "Yes. Yes, it is. And part of your heart, is it not? A piece of it is here in this castle, isn't it?"

"I've buried the memories of my time here," Mama says.

I shift my feet, trying to get my blood pumping again as it has felt stagnant since I came into the presence of the queen.

Phoenix turns her gaze to me. "I didn't even notice you. You must be the younger daughter."

It's not a question. She knows exactly who I am, but she doesn't want to acknowledge me. I glance at Mama, who's looking between the queen and me.

"Remove your cloak, child," Phoenix orders.

If I had more courage, I would say no. As much as I despise the queen, I'm scared. Or maybe I'm smart enough not to rebel right to her face. Slowly, I lower the hood.

Phoenix grins. "You look like a little red wraith, creeping into my castle, trying to hide your crescent eyes."

My stomach swoops like I'm falling off a horse. Will she kill me here in this room because she thinks I'm useless? A noise, a stopped word in someone's throat, gives me a small sense of comfort. It's Greyson, and I think it means he has my back. I can't explain why, but I feel it, and I trust it.

"Phoenix, don't you dare," Mama says lowly. "Leave my daughter alone."

Phoenix waves her hand and smiles. "Never mind that. I'll take a leaf out of your book and get straight to the point as to why I brought you here. I'm planning on naming an heir to the throne before I enact some new laws. You see, I need my subjects to know my line will not end, nor will my laws, even if they try to kill me." She laughs again like she's delivered a particularly witty punchline. Mama, Papi, Redford, and I must have missed the joke.

"What does your heir have anything to do with me or my family?" Mama snaps, making Phoenix's eyes gleam, the irises catching sparks from the fiery sconces that hang around the room.

"Oh, I think you'll agree it has *everything* to do with you and your family."

Phoenix nods to Greyson. He bows shortly and exits the room. Any sense of comfort I had with his presence departs with him, leaving me shaky and clammy.

Phoenix's blood-red nails tap her chin, surveying Mama. "It's too bad London couldn't be here."

Mama's gaze has never left Phoenix's. "How did you—" She swallows, her throat bobbing. I glance at Papi, wondering if Mama, too, has concluded that Phoenix must have grilled him about Mama.

"I buried her," Mama says, her voice strong and unafraid.

"You buried a body."

"Phoenix." Mama's voice breaks this time, sending terror through my bones. Of course we buried a body. We buried London's body. I know because I tried to heal it. I know because Redford pulled his ring from her finger. I know because I screamed for London, and if she'd had any life left in her, she would have answered.

The door opens again, and Greyson enters, his face expressionless. Someone moves behind him. A girl, not much older than me, dressed in a sapphire riding coat and black breeches, wearing a knight's helmet over her face, enters. Greyson bows to her.

"May I present," Phoenix says, grinning at Mama, "my

niece. London, princess of the warsol, heir to the Miadien throne. My Moonbeam."

Mama sinks to her knees. Papi, who's been silent this whole time, doesn't look shocked. Instead, tears stream down his face. He knew. He met this princess before we came.

I grasp Redford's elbow. "Galaxies above. This isn't real."

The girl removes her helmet. Black hair. Blue eyes. A scar slashed across her face that hadn't been there when she was alive. But there is no mistaking her.

My sister, London, has been raised from the dead.

NINE

ama falls forward, her face slamming into the stone floor. Seeing this ghost has made her faint, but I hope it hasn't done more. My heart pounds, almost ready to burst. Mama's likely broke in half.

Papi yells and rushes to her side. Redford helps Papi roll Mama over. Blood is smeared across her face.

"Greyson!" I scream. "Get help!" But he's already halfway out the door, going, I hope, to get a healer or someone who can help Mama.

"Anna!" My name is on the lips of London—this conjured-from-the-grave sister. I will not look at her. I cannot look at her.

Through it all, Phoenix just chuckles like she's watching an amusing play she's directing on a stage she built.

"My queen," London says, her voice sounding exactly the way I remember it, "it would be—"

"Yes, yes, my darling. You may help your mother."

London moves toward Mama, but I snarl at her, my canine teeth pulsing—the only physical reaction I've ever had that an animal could be inside me. "Stay away from my mother!"

Redford's arms go around me, holding me from what,

I'm not sure. Tearing out the queen's eyes? Slapping that cruel smile from her face? Or perhaps from flinging that cursed helmet back on the girl's head, that personification of my sister. I am London now, the daughter my parents need.

"She doesn't need you," I say, seething.

London stops dead, and Phoenix laughs again. It's lucky Greyson returns right at that moment, or else I would have clawed at Redford and flung myself onto the queen, consequences be damned.

Greyson returns, bringing two crowes who wear black uniforms with a red symbol embroidered on their sleeves. Healers possibly, but still crowes. Dark-feathered, usually with orange or red eyes with black sunburst pupils, and more angular than their distant paison cousins, they are nocturnal birds, night stalkers who keep watch over the warsol royalty in exchange for the warsol's protection in the Edges, the small part of Adderin that is not governed by the aeobanach in Istreya, but by the Crescent to the Moon Throne, Skoll.

"They'll take her to the infirmary," Greyson says, "where Skoll can see to her. Amethyst's skills are reserved only for royalty, but Skoll is more than capable."

No one says anything to Greyson. I keep my eyes trained on Mama until the crowes and Papi leave the room.

London tries to speak again, but Greyson, his voice low, says, "Give her time, Your Highness."

Redford's arms tighten around me again, not to prevent me from doing anything, but to let me know he's here, that he's hurting, that he doesn't believe this, either.

"Redford," she says softly, but he only grunts and shifts us away from her so we don't have to look at her.

She's been dead to us for over a year. We're seeing a ghost.

Her soft footsteps fade and then are gone, but I hear a choked sob before all goes silent. Like the grave.

"How?" I ask Greyson, turning back around. "That can't be her. My London wouldn't have let me believe she was dead."

"She will explain." Greyson forces his voice into what I assume he thinks is a placating tone. "You'll both need time—"

"She had time!"

"Not her own."

I stare at him, and Redford grunts again, the only sound he's been able to make.

"Come," Greyson says. "I'll show you to a room where you can rest. I promise you there will be explanations, but they are not mine to give."

We sit in plush chairs near a fire. We stay for hours, speaking up dozens of times to speculate how, why, when. To deny, explain, and argue. But we fall silent when we can't come up with any conclusions.

It's nearly midnight when the crowes bring Mama back and Papi follows in tow. A thick bandage covers Mama's face, and she's been put in an herb-induced sleep to ease the swelling and the pain. The healers say her head and face are fine. It's her heart they're more worried about, which is what I feared. Apparently, the shock of a ghost was almost more than she could bear.

Papi wraps me in a hug before climbing into bed next to Mama, finally allowing himself to sleep.

The room has four beds, one in each corner. Redford silently takes the one closest to the door. After Greyson brought us dinner and asked if we needed anything else, Redford had muttered something about needing a drink, but I ignored it, thinking that was the last thing he needed. Although, I think I understand it, the need to be numb. After all, his dead fiancée just turned up, all corporeal and breathing. I imagine what he must be thinking. He just wasted a proposal on the younger sister, the amorphous, when his incarnate fiancée has been alive this entire time.

Sleep doesn't find me the way it does my parents and Redford. I get out of bed and pace in front of the fireplace, which does nothing to ease my anxiety, so I make myself some chamomile tea with the herbs Greyson left in my pocket. The steam runs over my fingers, and I breathe in the scent, letting the herb calm me. When I finish the cup, I lean my head back, feeling slightly better, hoping I'll get sleepy.

But my thoughts are, as usual, on my sister. I saw her body, brushed the dark hair off her frozen, pale face. Kissed her hands and wept, wanting to crawl into the grave with her.

I can't stay in this stuffy room. I can't stay in this castle. But I can't leave, either. My parents' sleeping forms are black lumps across the room, the faint rise and fall of their chests the only movement that indicates they are alive. Redford's back is to me, so I crack open the door that leads to the castle corridor. I back out of the room, close the door quietly, and turn to a shadow in the corridor. A ghost.

"Anna," she says, the tone in her voice as strained and pained as it had been on a night that seems so long ago now. It was the night she'd woken me to tell me she'd accepted Redford's proposal.

"I want to marry him," she'd said. "I'm over the moon. But that means I'll have to leave you."

I'd hugged her tightly. "I'll be leaving anyway to become a healer."

"You'll be the best. And I won't be far. Redford and I want to build a cabin in the mountains."

"No, you won't be far," I'd replied. "We'll see each other all the time."

"I'll never leave you for good."

"But you did," I say out loud now, pulling my mind away from the past and focusing on the girl before me. The one who says she's my sister. Although Phoenix has crowes, practitioners of dark magic, bringing someone back from the dead isn't possible. Redford and I discussed that, mulled it over and strained it through all the combined knowledge we have of magic. Which isn't much. But the one fact we'd settled on was if someone can be brought back from the dead, Phoenix would have brought back dozens of warsol already, ones she had prized and valued. Her brother, Prince Falcon, would have been the first. She wants to rebuild the incarnate bloodline, after all.

London blinks at me, confused. "I did what?"

"You left me for good. If you've been alive all this time, why haven't you come home?"

"Anna," London says, her hands lowered and splayed by her hips, a gesture of surrender. "I have so much—"

She breaks off when I turn away and walk down the corridor, clenching my fists.

This puzzle has a lot of misplaced pieces. But the one thing I don't understand—apart from her miraculous resurrection—is that Phoenix had called London her niece. Redford theorized that Phoenix had likely convinced herself that she'd somehow legally adopted her, but as a niece, not a daughter. She is, after all, the actual daughter of an amorphous warsol, and we all know that Phoenix can't stomach the amorphous. I'd asked the knottiest question of all. Phoenix isn't Mama's sister, is she? No. She can't be.

"Anna, please," London says. "May I talk to you?"

I keep going. If I don't talk to her, if I don't acknowledge her presence—

"Anna."

How many nights had I wept for her? How many days had I done nothing but sit in one spot, wishing for her return? How many times had I wished she'd come back to life?

"You need to understand. I've done this for you."

I whip around. "You let me believe you were dead for my own good? I have mourned you for a year. It killed me when you died. *I* died. A part of me was gone, lost forever." Cracked words spoken by a broken voice, every syllable choked.

"I mourned it, too, Anna! I missed you every single moment of every day I've been away. But you'll never understand unless you let me explain."

I turn away from her again, crashing headlong into a solid gray wall.

"Excuse me, Anna." It's Greyson. "I'm sorry, Your Highness, but you know my orders."

London sighs and closes her eyes briefly. "You found me in record time."

He quirks up one silver eyebrow. "I was perched outside your room as if you were in there, but—"

"I know, I know. Her crowes scuttled by, and you had to hurry and find me before they did."

Greyson shrugs, and he glances at me, giving me a half-grin. Even in my distressed state, it still makes my heart flutter, my stomach flip-flop.

"Anna?" London ventures. "Will you walk with me? Please. Give me five minutes. I don't know when I'll have the chance—"

"Aren't you the *princess?*" The venom I inject into my voice seems to hit her in the face because she flinches.

"Five minutes?" is all she says.

"Fine." But then I fire my anger at Greyson. "Why didn't you tell me? You knew London was here, alive."

"Would you have believed me? A queen's soldier?"

He's right. I would have suspected it was a trick, a way to lure me away from the small sense of safety I'd built around my home.

"Talk to her," he says quietly and pushes me gently in London's direction. He follows us but from a respectable distance.

I'm careful not to even brush up against this princess. I keep eyeing her, though, because I'm afraid she'll vanish into thin air, like fog when it's burned off by the sun.

"Where should I start?" she asks.

I give a humorless laugh. "How will you ever explain how you came back from the dead?"

"That one is easy enough."

I raise my eyebrows and try not to scoff.

"Someone else took my place."

I stop. "That is not possible. She was you. She looked exactly like you. So, who is the black-magic imitation? You, the princess standing in front of me, or the one buried deep in the ground?"

"No one is buried there anymore."

"What do you—" Images invade my mind. The disturbed earth. The tilted headstone. Someone had dug their way out of the grave. Nauseated, I stop, bending with my hands on my knees, taking deep, slow breaths.

"Anna?" London says, hesitantly reaching to touch me, but I hold up one hand.

"This is too much," I say, gasping to keep my stomach from hurling its meager contents. My head spins. I lean against the stone wall, pressing a hand to the cold glass of a window.

And then Greyson is there, his arm around my waist, the other holding my hand. "Come on, Anna," he says, so softly I almost don't hear him. "You are exhausted, and you've had the shock of your life. You need to rest." He glances at London. "May I take her to her room, Your Highness?"

"Of course," she says, worry lacing her tone.

We make our way back down the corridor. London says to my retreating back, "But Anna, it is me. I can tell you anything you want from our past to prove it."

Anyone who wanted to impersonate my sister would have been studying, would have been focused on her. Watching us, like Greyson was watching me before he delivered the letter.

I wrench my body out of his hold.

"You. You spied on us, learned everything about her." I point a trembling finger at the princess. "About our family, before you killed—before you replaced—"

"It's not—" Greyson starts, but I've already shut the door in his face.

He, too, has betrayed me.

TEN

The disturbed grave was nothing more than an animal digging for an easy meal.

My London doesn't have a scar on her face.

Queen Phoenix is not our relative, so London can't possibly be her heir.

There is so much more damning evidence against this princess, but the crowning piece is that my London would not have let me believe she was dead. She wouldn't have let me drown in my sorrow.

Sunlight streams into the room, but sleep didn't touch my eyes. I sat up in the bed, leaning against the wall, watching my parents sleep.

Redford rolls over, his eyes opening slightly. He peers at me and grins, but I see the memory of yesterday rushing at him like a tidal wave. His lips curve downward, and his brow furrows. Then, the movement that breaks me—he covers his face with his hands and breathes slowly. I have only seen Redford cry once.

I get out of my bed and slip into his, wrapping one arm around his torso. He lowers his hands and clutches my arm.

There is something kindred in the sharing of the same kind of hurt, to have been betrayed by the same person.

"I'm leaving," he says.

It's not like I didn't expect this. He needs to get back to his own family, but something tightens in my gut at the thought of not having him with me. Of having to fight this battle alone, just like all the nights he spent at the pub rather than with me when I needed him the most.

I didn't realize how hurt I'd been by that until now. He's been a comfort, a friend, a soul in loss. It's not just that I don't want him to leave. I don't want to lose him.

"Are you going to talk to her?" I ask, my voice thick with hurt, or dread, or something akin to both.

His throat bobs up and down, just once. "There is nothing to say. She chose a throne over me. Over *us*. She let us believe she was dead. It's not as if she'd be allowed to marry me, anyway."

A flash of something knifes across my gut. Is it jealousy? "So, you... you still want to. To marry her."

"No," he says, his voice sounding strangled by his pain. He sits, and my arm falls away, so I sit, too, but he climbs over me and excuses himself to go to the privy. His back muscles contract, bowing his spine forward slightly. His shoulders are lifted as if he's shrugging. He walks hunched in his hurt.

The door closes behind him, and I slide back down into his bed, pulling the blankets over my shoulders. When he comes out, he gathers his belongings, and I watch him pack, owl-eyed, peering over the top of the blankets. He goes back into the privy to dress. When he comes out again, he takes longer than necessary to retrieve his bag. My heart aches that he won't be sleeping here tonight. Won't be here with me.

He comes to me, and I crawl out from underneath the blankets. I wrap my arms around his waist.

"Tell your parents goodbye," he says.

"Will I see you again?" He takes a deep breath, but before he can speak, I cut in. "You can take it back, you know."

He tilts his head, studying me, his brown eyes searching mine. His rough hands cup my face, and he leans close to me. "I don't want to take it back."

We stare at each other for a few heart-pounding moments. I want to say yes, but so many thoughts fight for precedence in my brain. But the one I voice is, "I won't be allowed to marry you, Redford. Phoenix will sign the law, and clearly, London is doing nothing to stop it."

"It's not law yet," Redford points out.

I lean my forehead against his. Is he my one chance at happiness? Marry now, or never marry. Finding and falling in love with another amorphous is a possibility, but do I even want to marry and have children who would be spurned in this wretched kingdom? Does it even matter if the castle sanctions our marriage or not? We could just live together, in friendship, in… love.

But there is the reality of Greyson. There had been something there, that is still there, even though I believe him to be in league with my sister and the queen. If I marry Redford, a gray ghost will haunt the back of my mind because of the burning in my chest when I look at him, think of him.

Our time to figure this out is limited. So, I make an excuse, one to hold Redford at bay because I don't want to lose him, but I don't know how to make him stay.

"I need to find out what my parents—I need to know if they're staying here. Can I meet you at the skeleton tree by the end of the week?"

An expression flashes over Redford's face I can't quite place. Hurt. Confusion. Both. But he nods, kisses me lightly on the cheek, and goes to the door. I follow him out, and he turns around.

"You should know I still love her. Who she was. And I miss her. But it's you, now, who has claimed my heart." His fingers slip into my hair, running them through the strands. "I wouldn't want you ever to think I settled for you."

But he can't hide the hurt in his eyes, deep and dark like a trench, and I know he, too, will be haunted by someone else, even while sharing a life with me.

He drops his hand from my hair and cups the back of my head. "It would be unfair, though, if I didn't tell you that by marrying me"—he leans forward as if he's going to kiss me, but at the last second, he slides his lips to my ear and whispers—"you'll be marrying a rebel."

I jerk back and stare at him. Certainly, neither of us have agreed with Phoenix's laws, and we have always crusaded for equal rights for the amorphous. What does he mean that he's a rebel? Is he in some secret group that flagrantly fights the queen? Are they the ones who burned the villages near the castle?

"The man at the inn," I whisper.

"My captain," Redford replies. "He wanted me to stay rather than come with you."

"Why didn't you?"

He shakes his head, and I understand. Not here, not in the castle.

"I will see you at the skeleton tree," he says and walks away.

I wrap my arms tightly around my waist, holding back this aching, empty feeling as he leaves.

In this castle, I'm shunned for being amorphous. But only briefly. Because whoever looks down their snout at me then finds out I'm Princess London's unfortunate amorphous sister. I'm not given respect or apologies, only a wide berth. I can't decide if being ignored or snarled at is better.

I leave the room to clear my head, get some fresh air, and I sense someone behind me. I don't even have to turn to know who it is. He doesn't avoid me when he sees me coming. In fact, he seeks me out. He smells like chamomile and wood-smoke tinged by lavender. The scent sends a thrill up my spine, hard as I try to fight it.

"My lady," he says.

Anger, sharp like claws, rips through me. We are not royal, and I don't want that title. I snarl. "Isn't your job to guard the princess, Greyson?"

"I've come at the request of the princess, Anna. She would like to meet with you in her chambers."

"I'd rather not."

"I didn't think you'd be amenable to it."

"But you won't leave me alone until I go, right?" I turn around as Greyson shrugs. "I don't even know where her chambers are."

"Luckily for you, I have come as your escort."

My teeth grind as I tighten my jaw to stop myself from snarling at him again. I close my eyes briefly. "Yes, I figured you would."

"I don't think you like me very much, Anna."

I snort. "You don't say."

Expecting a tart response, I move ahead, not wanting to talk to him anymore. When he doesn't follow, I glance back. He looks straight ahead, shoulders stiff, back rigid.

I raise my eyebrows. "Well? Are you escorting me, or can I go do as I please?"

He shifts his eyes so his silver-moon gaze meets mine. "You can try, but you won't get far in this castle." He walks toward me but doesn't stop. He continues down the corridor, and I reluctantly follow, knowing he's right. If I tried to go anywhere without an escort, I'd be put straight to work as an amorphous servant—or worse, prison—until they figured out who I was, of course. In that case, they'd send me immediately to my sister.

"So, do you believe London is who she says she is? You don't believe she's being Assumed?" Greyson asks.

"I don't know what that means." My tone is warm like coals, but it lacks the red-hot fury it had moments ago.

He glances at me. "Assumption—being Assumed—is a complex magic that involves taking on the appearance of someone else. It was discovered by Branwyn."

I scowl. "Of course it was a crowe. So, by the use of magic, someone can look like someone else?"

Greyson nods.

"So, is she Assumed?"

"No."

"Then why mention it if you believe she's the real London?"

Greyson glances around—up to the ceiling, over his shoulder, behind me. Then, he laughs, but there is no real joviality behind it, although also no meanness.

"I find it...." Greyson pauses, and as he does, two castle guards round the corner.

They stop abruptly, straighten their stances, and salute Greyson. "Captain," they say, almost in unison.

Greyson nods at them, then says, "Proceed." His tone is cold like late autumn air, but it also seems unaffected. The guards continue down the hallway, and Greyson says, "As I was saying, I find it amusing that the amorphous are so uninformed about what magic can and cannot do."

One of the soldiers stifles a laugh as they continue down the corridor. I wish his words had made me angry, but instead I'm hurt. I recoil, both from him and from my wounded pride. Who cares if he, too, thinks amorphous are worthless?

He clears his throat. "Sorry," he whispers.

I glance at the soldiers' retreating backs. He didn't say that for their benefit to make them think that *he* thinks the way they do.

"We better get you to the princess."

I follow silently. I want to ask him about what just happened. Why he said it, why he had to pretend, if that's what he was doing. But it seems like these walls are thin or have ears of their own. Instead, I ask, "How did you get the bruise? It wasn't from training."

Greyson glances back at me. "Some of the guards were a bit rougher than I would have preferred when we captured your father. A blow landed on me as I tried to protect him."

I stop. "You shielded my father?"

"Yes."

"Why?"

"He's not a prisoner who has committed any crimes."

"Except to be amorphous."

"That's not a crime."

"Just an unfortunate state-of-being."

"I didn't say that."

"No," I agree. "You didn't. But we amuse you with our lack of knowledge. Which, by the way, is untrue. Plenty of amorphous know and study magic."

He stops and turns fully around. We stare at each other, and he takes a deep, shaky breath. "Not like the incarnate."

His statement is loaded, but he doesn't let me unpack it with my questions.

"Two summers ago," he says quietly as he starts to walk again, "my father brought me to the castle for a season. He was a queen's guard, barely involved in our lives except to send money and provisions. I was no use to him until I was old enough to be a soldier. I proved to be talented in fighting and scouting, so I was promised a lifelong wage if I took my father's place when he retired. I couldn't say no to a steady income to support my mother and brother."

I have no idea why he's telling me this. I don't want to care, but I find myself interested in his backstory, what brought him to the service of this awful queen. "Did he?"

"Did he what?"

"Your father. Did he retire?"

Greyson shakes his head. "He died."

"Oh—I'm sorry." I think that I actually *am* sorry, but I'm also angry again. If he lost someone he loved, why did he play a part in making another person believe their loved one was dead?

"He was more like an uncle who was distantly fond of his nephews as long as they served a purpose. But I didn't necessarily want to have my father's position."

"What was it?"

"The queen's captain."

I frown. That would have been a high honor for someone so young. But before I can ask why, Greyson says, "I volunteered to be the princess's personal guard."

His words weigh heavily on me, so much so that I have to straighten my back to continue walking. I can't decipher the double connotation. Why? Why did he want London? Why does anyone want *my* London when I need her so badly?

I remind myself *my* London is dead and gone, and if anyone has Assumed her, it's me.

"Here are your sister's rooms," Greyson says, stopping my thoughts. "I will be outside." He raps on the door lightly, then stands back into the shadows of the corridor.

A part of me—the part I'm trying to fight, the part I'm trying to subdue—wants to stay out here with him. Maybe to be with him. Maybe to hide from the person inside the room. I don't know yet. I don't know if I ever will know.

The door creaks open and, feeling like I'm going to court, prison, or even the Underearth, I square my shoulders, lift my chin, and go inside.

ELEVEN

Princess London is situated in a throne-like chair in her opulent room. The chair is deep indigo, the same color as the velvet curtains that spill over her canopied bed. A fire roars behind a grate, and dinner is on the table. My stomach betrays me by growling, clawing for whatever is laid out.

"Anna," London says, her voice clear as bells and clanging with joy. "I'm so happy you're here."

I don't reply, and London nods as if she understands why I'm silent. She could never hope to understand. She's never buried me, never tried to get over the loss of her best friend, her guiding star, her true North.

London stands. "I know you're hurting, Anna. But you must believe me that I have mourned you as much as you have mourned me."

A sharp, flinty laugh jumps from my mouth. "Is that so? You knew I was alive. You knew you'd see me again."

London's temples bounce as if she's grinding her jaw. "Perhaps." Her teeth glint in the semi-dark, and she looks as feral as Phoenix. Nausea rolls inside me as if I'm on a wave-tossed ship, and I shiver. Her tone is a mimicry of Phoenix's, another fact that solidifies she belongs to the queen now.

I knew the moment she took off the helmet. Again, the truth hits me like a fist. My London is gone.

"Please sit," she says, gesturing to the well-set table. "I'm starving, and I don't want to try to explain everything over my growling stomach."

The barest hint of a smile touches my mouth, remembering the way my sister would be angrier than all the wolves in a den when she was hungry. She'd lose her cool so fast, she'd sprout her wolf fangs and ears and bang around the kitchen until the first bite hit her stomach. Then, she'd eat faster than any of us and sigh in complete contentment when her plate was empty.

I can't deny my stomach any longer, either, so I take a seat opposite London's throne-like one, putting a shaking hand on my forehead. She sits across from me and reaches as if to touch me but draws back when I curl my lip at her. I'm still not ready for that.

London begins eating first, so I follow suit, trying not to glance at her every time I put my fork in my mouth. After several minutes, London sighs, that same satisfied breath of a well-fed wolf that I remember, and leans back in her chair.

"I did get in an accident on Lassiter. That's how I got this ugly scar. He's still mine. Greyson captured him for me, and he has a royal stall here at the castle."

I want to run my hands over the white mark to assure her it doesn't diminish her beauty, but I fist my hands, wishing I had talons like the crowes to dig into my skin and remind myself not to fall for anything this reincarnation of my sister says.

"But when I woke up, I wasn't in the woods anymore, and I wasn't home. I was here in the castle, and Phoenix was tending to me. She told me about my accident. She rescued me from the woods."

She looks at me from the corner of her eye, something she

used to do when she was lying to get us out of trouble when we were kids. What is she lying about right now? Everything?

A raven caws, and I jump, noticing for the first time the bird perched in London's windowsill. It cocks its head at me, its black eyes reflecting orange in the firelight.

"It's okay, Eddy," London says soothingly to the bird. She goes over to him and gives him crumbs from her plate, running a slim finger over his glossy black feathers.

Eddy turns up his beak at me as if to say, "She loves *me* now."

"I asked to have Mama come," London says. "Phoenix told me she'd send for Mama as soon as I was ready."

"Ready for what?"

"I didn't know it at the time, but she meant when I had accepted who I was. That I was her heir." London takes a deep breath. "You see, Anna, I *am* her niece. Mama was married to Prince Falcon years ago."

"That's ridiculous." I actually laugh, and Eddy squawks at the sudden sharp sound coming from my mouth. "It's just another lie."

London sits back at the table and folds her hands in her lap, looking down at them. "I didn't believe it at first, either." She brings her head back up, eyes shining with tears. "But Phoenix has their marriage certificate and showed me the official records of marriage and of my birth. I'm Falcon's child, not Papi's. I look...." She pushes back from the table and goes to a chest of drawers near her bed. "I look like Falcon." She pulls out a scroll, then comes over and hands it to me.

I avoid her gaze as I unroll the parchment. It's all there. Everything she said. Mama's marriage to Falcon, dated nineteen years prior. London's birth, dated shortly after. A quick sketch of the bride and groom on their wedding day.

A sudden burning sensation fills my entire core. It's not that this knowledge—if it's actually true, if it's not a forged document—changes how I feel about what makes us family. There are bonds stronger than blood. It's Mama's—and really,

Papi's, too—secrecy that hurts. They didn't trust us with the truth. Did they think it would have changed how we felt about each other? Sisters are sisters, bound by blood or something else. Something stronger.

"Mama fled the castle with me, then kept me hidden from Phoenix. That's why we've always lived near the border and why Mama always forbade us to get involved in royal affairs. But Phoenix said she'd heard rumors of her once-sister-in-law and her children. How one was dark and incarnate and the other crimson and amorphous. She sent Greyson's father to spy on us and took her chance when I was alone. Greyson's father brought me here, traded my body for one in the woods."

My fork clangs against the plate. London doesn't even flinch at the noise.

"He told me his father died."

"He did, shortly after."

"Of natural causes?"

She quirks up her eyebrow. "No. A skirmish at the border. Amorphous were trying to get into Adderin, and Istreya doesn't want a mass immigration."

"Maybe the amorphous wouldn't want to leave if we were treated fairly."

Eddy flaps his wings, his hideous caw echoing around the room. London goes to him and soothes him again. She looks out the window for a long time, stroking Eddy's feathers and staring in the distance.

London's voice is slightly farther away when she speaks again. "I love Papi. He is my father, and being Falcon's child doesn't mean I'm not Papi's daughter. It just means I have Falcon's blood. Papi has my love. But it does mean I'm Phoenix's niece and heir."

I close my eyes to stop the spinning. Falcon died years ago, before London was even born. He was the crown prince. Phoenix was never meant to be the queen, but she became the heir when Falcon was slayed.

"The murdered prince," I say.

London cocks her head. "The queen maintains that opinion, but the official record shows that," her voice is closer now, and I open my eyes, seeing she has returned to the table, "he was killed in a battle between the incarnate and amorphous soldiers of the king." The king had just outlawed amorphous from serving in his ranks. Phoenix shared her father's sentiments against the amorphous, even more so after her brother was killed."

"And now she's about to sign in a law that will prevent amorphous from marrying. And you, her heir, agree with her?"

London just looks at me. Her gaze darts once to Eddy, but then they're fixed back on me. "I would not have stayed if I didn't agree." She says the words carefully as if she's stepping on them like stones in a stream, one by one.

The words sting almost as badly as her death. My sister—my hero—thinks I'm useless.

TWELVE

 shape shifts in the darkest corner of the room. At first, I think she's a dark blue paison, but then I notice the differences. Sharper facial angles, pitch-black feathers, eyes like molten lava, talons the hue of soot. A crowe. She glides over to London as if she's flying, clutching a carafe in her talons. Her eyes don't meet mine as she fills my glass.

London says, "This is Branwyn."

What does she want me to say to the crowe? It's nice to meet her? I'm glad she's a servant to the princess?

Branwyn saves me from saying anything, though, because she merely nods and glides away, back into the darkness. One of her wings is bent as if it had been broken and healed at an awkward angle.

"Did you know the crowes can hold their breath for days?" London asks.

I scowl. The crowes, it was rumored, had once been able to do that because they lived near the sea. The tides would come into their caves, where they lived like bats, and in order to survive, learned to hold their breath for long periods of time. I never knew if that was true or only a story, and anyway, I don't care. The crowes are only kept in check from tearing our eyes out while we sleep because of the warsol's guardianship over them. They aren't the friendliest of creatures and prefer to stick with their own kind. But Miadien lets them have a semi-autonomous role in the Edges. The Crescent merely makes certain they don't get too independent because they are terrifying fighters, allies the queen cherishes. I'm sure they will be loosed on the amorphous soon, though. It won't take much time for Phoenix to decide that because we can't marry, we have no purpose, so we may as well not live.

"I don't really care what the crowes can and cannot do. What I do care about is that you show up from the dead and tell me you now believe in something you were always against. The mistreatment of the amorphous."

Eddy flutters over and lands in the middle of the table, pecking at the leftover food. London's gaze flicks between him and me. He is, by far, the strangest bird I have ever seen.

"You will come to understand—" London begins.

"No. I won't."

She takes a deep breath. "If you believe I am who I say I am—"

I laugh. "Right. Explain that, then. Why are you allowed to show yourself now? Why couldn't the queen have just come and talked to Mama instead of making us believe you were dead?"

"Do you really think Mama would have let me go? That I would have come here willingly? Phoenix and Mama have bad blood between them, but that shouldn't stop me from taking my rightful place on the throne. Phoenix stole me, yes, but she took care of me, told me the truth of who I am. Mama has lied to me all these years."

"So, that's it? Phoenix has you for one year, and everything Mama and Papi ever did for you is worthless?"

"I didn't say that."

"You didn't have to."

"Phoenix didn't want to let Mama know until I had fully

accepted who I am. Until I was ready to refuse Mama's request to go home. This is my home now, Anna. And also, keeping my family in the dark gave me a reason to stay. To know one day she'd let me bring you all here."

"Stay? In this incarnate-infested castle where they—*you*—think amorphous are worthless?"

"Phoenix believes in order to make our race strong, we need more incarnate. The crowes are getting stronger, and—"

"I hope they overrun you," I say, surprised at the poison out of my mouth, surprised I dare speak up, surprised I have any spine at all.

"Anna."

"When will you incarnate ever understand you can't rule over everyone who you think is weaker than you?"

"The crowes—"

"I know the history," I interrupt. "I know their ancestors made deals with the warsol to avoid being enslaved by the aeo-banach, but more so, to avoid being *eaten* by you animals. To have a facade of freedom in the Edges."

London looks as if I've slapped her. A pain hits me in my chest, and I wish I could take back the words. But she is the queen's heir. The queen who hates my kind.

Eddy squawks loudly.

"You have made your position quite clear, Anna." London blinks rapidly, but since she never cries, I doubt it's tears she's wiping away. She takes a deep breath. "Allow me to make one more plea. Stay in the castle. I can protect you when the war comes. Because it is coming, Anna. Rebels are already fighting the law."

I think about Redford and his rebellious actions. The once-lovers will be pitted against each other in a war, I think bitterly. I have a choice in front of me. I can stand next to my sister or with my kind.

My kind is warsol. It shouldn't have to be incarnate or amorphous.

"Of course it is," I say lowly. "The amorphous won't just sit back and let Phoenix oppress them."

"Phoenix's army is too powerful. The amorphous will cause their own genocide if they fight. And I could use your help, Anna, to try to change things."

"My help? What can I do?"

"Your knowledge of plants—"

"I gave that up when you died."

London stops. After a few short breaths, she says, "I'm alive again. You should be, too. You could pick it back up. I need to create a potion or serum or something—" She pauses, noticing how I'm looking away. "Give me a chance, Anna." The last sentence is a whisper, a prayer.

I shake my head. "I still don't understand. Why did you let us believe you were dead? Why couldn't you have sent us a message? Why make us go through your death?"

London lowers her eyes, the black lashes brushing her pale cheeks as she blinks. "Because the London you knew did die."

"Well," I say, trying to act as if the hurt isn't deeper than the grave we dug, "Mama, Papi, and I have died a little more each day since you've been gone. Maybe I should have crawled in that grave with you." London goes to speak, but I hold up my hand. "I don't want to hear anymore. You're right. My sister, London, is dead. You are not her."

My hands are trembling, and I glance down at them, at the gold wolf-and-fox ring cutting into the skin on my finger. Shaking, I wrench it off and toss it to London, who catches it with the hand that wears her own silver sister-ring.

The one we buried her with.

THIRTEEN

ama's sigh is like the breath of burgeoning spring. She must be overjoyed at having her incarnate daughter back. No matter what I did, I never could have replaced London or lived up to her. She's incarnate, and even though our parents always treated us as equals, I will always be amorphous, always be less. And now, I can't hope to be seen in my sister's resurrected shadow. I can't live up to coming back to life.

"Anna," Papi says as I close the door to our room behind me, "we assumed you were with London. How… how was it?"

I glance between my parents.

"Redford's gone," I say in response.

Mama and Papi share their own glance now.

"We figured he would go," Papi says softly. "I wanted to give him my thanks for helping to bring you both to me. To us."

"What was it like for you, Papi?" I ask, sitting on Mama's bed where she rests. "To see her again?"

Papi trembles slightly as he takes a seat next to me.

"It was… unbelievable. But that is our girl. Our London. She didn't need to prove it to me."

"Because you know she's Phoenix's niece." I can't keep the accusatory barb out of my tone.

My parents share another glance.

"We only withheld that from you girls to protect you," Papi says, as if throwing up a wall to protect Mama from anything I might say in anger.

"I know."

"You must be so angry with us," Mama whispers.

I am. I'm angry, I'm confused, but most of all, I'm—

"Hurt?" Mama's voice captures my thoughts. Her fingers intertwine with mine.

I don't trust my voice, so I just nod.

"I wanted to shield you both," Mama says.

"I know," I say again, but I find I don't want to talk about that. "What happened, Papi? Did you get hurt? Are you okay?"

He runs a hand over his tired face. "I'm not hurt. The guards tried to beat me into submission, but the captain, that gray soldier—"

"Greyson," I say immediately, then clamp my mouth shut.

"Yes. He seems to have some good character in him. He made them stop, threatened to demote them or dismiss them if they didn't treat me with general respect. None of them offered why I was being taken, though, other than my capture had been ordered by the queen. But I knew it had to do with your mother. I never dreamed it would be your sister."

"When did you see her?"

"She came to my cell the next morning. I nearly had heart failure. She begged the queen to let me out of the cell and be taken to a room. I wasn't mistreated, but I wasn't told much. London and I were never left alone. The queen simply said, 'I guess you know why I have her.'"

As if I've received a punch to the stomach, I double over, thinking how Papi must have felt when he heard that from the queen.

"London wants us to stay," Mama whispers.

I look at Papi. "And you?"

"My place is by your mother, so I will stay where she is."

"You'll stay right in this den of the incarnate where you're mistreated for being what you are?"

"I understand why this frightens you, Anna, but as I said, I wasn't mistreated."

"Because you're London's father! What happens when the incarnate win?"

"Anna," Mama says, "it will be an adjustment—"

"Maybe we don't *want* an adjustment!"

Mama's tone is flat but firm. "They stand no chance against the incarnate and their crowe allies."

"Maybe they have allies, too."

Mama, who had rested her head back on her pillow, brings it up to eye me. "I suspect there are pockets of rebel groups scattered throughout the country, but Anna, they cannot win. The best hope for the amorphous is the princess."

I can't believe what I'm hearing. We've had London back for one day, and suddenly we're on the incarnate's side, choosing to serve them because my once-dead sister is their princess. I know I should trust her, I should believe she has a plan, but I don't know the princess. I don't know this new sister.

"She told me the London we knew died," I say.

"In order to survive," Mama replies, "I believe she did. She is trying to find a way to make amorphous become incarnate so they won't—"

"What?" I interrupt. "She wants to change us? Why not just let us be who we are?" So, that was it. What London was asking me to do. She wanted to use my knowledge of plants to help her make a potion to change the amorphous, to force them to become incarnate.

My hands shake, and my back sweats, the contents of my stomach nearly coming up.

Something taps at the window, and Eddy, London's raven, stares at us with his beady black eyes.

The distraction quells my nausea but not my anger.

Mama and Papi look at each other, their expressions full of meaning that seems connected to a memory. One that has never been shared with me.

"Why don't we get some sleep?" Papi suggests as he helps Mama lie back down. "There will be plenty of time to talk in the coming days."

Nothing can be said that hasn't already been discussed. They are completely convinced London is who she says she is and that she has a plan to save everyone.

By changing the amorphous.

My throat aches, and my eyes water as I crawl in the bed Redford slept in the night before. I thought I had done the right thing when I decided to follow in London's footsteps, when I decided to think like her. But now she's back, and she's not the same London, and the only need anyone has for me is to help change my fellow amorphous into incarnate. To make us disappear.

FOURTEEN

he black curtain of night holds back the dawn when I leave a note on the bedside table and slip out of our chambers.

When it became apparent I wouldn't be able to change, our parents didn't compare my sister and me or tell me to try harder. Papi, in particular, was pleased that he wasn't going to be the only amorphous in the house. But I was ashamed because I wanted to be like Mama and London. I was ashamed because I didn't want to be like Papi.

But most of all, I was ashamed that I hated myself and the body I'd been born into. This past year with London gone, I had a lot of time to think about who I was without her, and the one thing that made me feel powerful, be seen, was to become like her.

I don't want to become like her anymore.

In the line between night and morning, I tread quietly through the castle corridors. But of course it can't be this easy because, as he always does, Greyson finds me.

"Anna," he says, his voice softer than the breaths of the sleeping occupants in the castle.

I close my eyes briefly. "Please don't stop me," I whisper. "I can't stay."

"You're not a prisoner," he says, "but an honored guest."

I give one short, humorless laugh. "I'm still leaving. I believe I outwore my welcome before I even stepped foot in this wretched place."

"I—" He clears his throat. "So many here want you to stay. Your sister won't allow anything to happen to you."

"But that's just it, Greyson. She forced me to live without her for a year, to believe she was dead. She can't protect me anymore because I don't need protecting. I shouldn't have to be protected from the warsol. I *am* warsol."

"The incarnate—"

"Have created an unnecessary division between our race. I'm going somewhere that I will be treated fairly, not because the princess requires it."

Greyson bows his head. "Where will you go?"

"I—" I pause. "Home."

"You're so young to be alone."

"I will be close to friends."

This time, Greyson pauses. "The red wolf?"

"Redford. Yes."

"Ah."

The silence between us is a pendulum swinging, a time clock ticking, until I say, "Thank you for the clothes and the herbs."

"Thank you for healing my bruise."

"How did you find clothing that fit me so well?"

"My mama makes all different sizes. I chose the ones I thought would fit you best."

"You chose perfectly."

Greyson leans closer. "Anna, I—"

The soft hush of feathers brushing along stone floor makes us pause and look toward the sound. Branwyn comes around the corner. She gives me a small nod, then says to Greyson, "The queen will be awakened in another hour and join the

Crescent for a breakfast meeting. I'd be happy to escort Anna to dine with her sister."

"I don't—" I start, but Greyson clears his throat.

"I believe the princess plans on eating breakfast at her favorite bakery outside the castle."

Branwyn raises her eyebrows, which are, fittingly, feathery. Her charcoal-gray hair is long and curly, and I think she'd be beautiful if she didn't have those strange orange eyes. But who am I to be disparaging against someone's eyes? Mine have crescent pupils, a sure sign that I am unable to change. "I see. Well, then, if you'll follow me, Anna."

I glance at Greyson, and he nods slightly. "Okay," I say.

She glides down the corridor, slightly ahead of me, and I glance back only once at Greyson, although his image is permanently imprinted in my mind. I don't imagine I'll ever be able to forget the way his silver hair shines like a slice of the moon, or the way his gaze landed on me like stardust.

"Through here," Branwyn says, opening a door on the left. We enter another corridor, this one dark as pitch, and Branwyn closes the door. My night vision flickers on, and I whip around, thinking she has shut me in, but she's right behind me. A blow as sharp and swift as Papi's axes when he chops wood nearly splits me open, and I almost think it's literal, the pain is so real. I should have told Greyson goodbye. I should have told him something. Anything. Everything.

Branwyn moves around me, the silhouette of her crooked wing disappearing down the steep pathway, so I follow, stumbling over stones. As I near her, I trip and knock into her back, catching her by her feathers and landing in a ridiculous heap at her feet.

"I'm sorry," I gasp, clutching my side.

Branwyn doesn't say anything, only offers her taloned hand to help me up. Her touch is surprisingly soft.

We continue in silence until I can't stand it anymore.

"Where are we going?" I whisper, massaging my rib.

"To breakfast, of course."

"Umm...."

"We have to go through the tunnels. It's a public place, and she is the princess. We cannot just waltz in there like regular patrons."

"Right. But—"

Branwyn stops and turns. She cocks her head bird-like and cuts me off by placing her taloned finger to her lips. She points at the ceiling, but even with my night vision, I can't see anything.

But above me, I hear the soft flapping of wings. After a few more minutes, I clear my throat, hoping she'll understand I'm asking if I can talk again.

"Yes?" She remains facing forward.

"How did you break your wing?"

Her shoulders shake as if she's laughing. "I was born with it."

"So... you... you can't fly? You've never flown?"

"Unless you count flying from the nest I was born in." She chuckles darkly, and it echoes behind us, bouncing back toward the castle in an eerie refrain.

Natural light is ahead, and when we exit the tunnel, we are not only outside the castle walls, but also outside of the capital city limits. A raven—Eddy, I knew it—flies out of the tunnel, but Branwyn lifts her one good wing and clips him, knocking him to the ground. He rolls over and struggles to his little taloned feet.

"Oh, my darling," Branwyn coos, picking him up like he's a treasured pet or even a child. "Are you all right?"

I swear the blasted bird scowls at her.

Branwyn looks past me. "Oh, Greyson."

My heart leaps. He sits on a horse, but it's not his horse. It's my Berne.

"Would you mind escorting Anna the rest of the way to our princess's favorite breakfast spot? I've hurt dear Eddy."

"Yes, certainly."

"Thank you, Greyson," Branwyn says, cuddling the horrid raven to her chest.

Eddy turns his scowl on me, still looking a bit dazed.

Branwyn looks at me, and for a moment, I think she is London because her visage becomes the sister's that I have known all my life. Except the scar. That is new. But then it fades, although I keep seeking the familiar lines of her face. But she is Branwyn again, and I must have only imagined it. She nods at me, but before I can return the gesture or say anything, she is swallowed by the tunnel.

Greyson dismounts and hands me the reins.

I throw an arm around Berne's fuzzy neck. "Hello, boy." I keep my face buried for a few seconds, delaying the moment I have to face Greyson and all the things I want to say. All the things I can't say.

"You better go before the sun rises," he says softly.

I lean away from my horse and don't make eye contact. I put my boot in the stirrup and haul myself into the saddle. Only then do I look at him.

"It won't be this way forever," he says.

I swallow. "Maybe not. But it's this way now."

"The warsol…. We won't always be split. Your sister—"

"I don't want to hear about her anymore."

He stuffs his hands in his coat pockets. "I understand." He focuses on the horizon, where gray is pushing its way over the sun. "Avoid the main roads."

"I will."

He studies me for a few seconds. "You know, you have a knack for not being seen when you don't want to be."

I blink at him. "No, I don't. I'm just not seen."

He nods as if he understands. "That's what I mean. You don't want to be seen."

"Why wouldn't I want to be?"

"Well." He runs his fingers though his beautiful silver hair, and I have to fight the urge to slide my own fingers into the tresses. "Perhaps it's more that you have always been overshadowed, and because of that, you remain in a shadow-like state so no one sees you clearly. When I was at your cottage—"

"When you were trespassing," I say, correcting him.

"Queen's guards can't trespass." His response is automatic as if he's been trained to say so. He gives me a rueful grin. "Anyway, I didn't see you hiding by the tree. I only saw Redford."

"Maybe the problem isn't me," I retort. "Perhaps no one looks at me."

"I'm looking at you."

"I—" I break off with my mouth open slightly. Berne paws the ground, eager to go, and I tighten my grip on the reins. "I better go, Greyson."

"Anna, I—I wish we had time. I wish—" He clears his throat. "When this is over, can I find you?"

"Will this ever be over?" I ask, looking into his mesmerizing gray eyes.

Deep thunder from far off rolls across the sky, bringing a gust of cool air that ruffles my hair.

Greyson lifts his face to the direction of the wind. Not looking at me, he asks, "What's your favorite color?"

I don't even have to think about it. "Gray."

We look at each other and stare for a few long seconds, but then he nods, pats my horse's neck, and I turn toward home.

FIFTEEN

s it had on our journey to the castle, the rain joined me, and now I am soaking wet. I stop at the Lamplight Inn, even though it is on a major thoroughfare. Berne is exhausted, and I'm freezing.

As much as the warmth beckons me, though, I avoid the fireplace where Greyson gave me dry clothing. I even avoid the pub because memories of the way Redford looked at me across the tables play through my mind as if I'm rereading a favorite book. As I cast around for other subjects to think about, the only one that catches is London, and I can't think about her. I won't.

I go to my room, alone, grateful for the fire and hot bath waiting for me. I climb into the tub and lay my head back, forcing myself to think of other things. Like about how Mama and Papi must have reacted when they found my note. How I feel betrayed by the one person I trusted most. How her support of Phoenix's disgusting laws burns through me to my core, setting fire to anger and hurt that must have been smoldering since the day London died. I hope they understand I have never felt more alone in my life, even with my sister returned to life.

☾

A lantern flickers in our cottage as it comes into view-ing distance. I jerk to a halt, tugging on Berne's reins harder than I mean to.

"Sorry, boy," I murmur, stroking his neck. It could just be Redford making sure everything is okay. I ride to the skeleton tree and slip out of the saddle, doing my best to be as quiet as possible in case it's not Redford lurking in my home.

I creep toward the house and peer through the window. The figure inside isn't Redford. He's shorter and younger, al-though he's an incarnate wolf, too—I can tell by his suspended state—with brown hair and yellow eyes.

He chooses that moment to turn toward the window, and I don't have time to hide. But I remember what Greyson said to me when I left the castle. I can avoid being seen when I want to. The young incarnate trespassing in my home doesn't look harmless, necessarily, and he certainly doesn't belong in my home, but he's so young. I pull up my hood and crouch as he moves toward the window to peer outside.

Don't see me.

His yellow gaze grazes over my head and fixes on Berne. His brow furrows, and he moves out of sight. Seconds later, he's outside, walking toward my gelding, not even noticing me bent down below the window. He attempts to pet the horse with his clawed hands, but Berne shies away. He drops his arm and, in the bruised light of dusk, his profile looks even younger than I thought.

I stand. "Why were you in my house?"

The boy jumps, and he actually clutches his chest in a way I imagine an old woman would. It's so ridiculous that I crack a smile that I try to smother immediately.

"Are you Anna?"

My eyebrows shoot up. He must sense he's caught me off-guard because he grins, showing fanged teeth. Something is familiar about him, perhaps the angle of his jaw or the tilt of his smile, but I can't place it.

"Where did you come from?" he asks.

"I think I should be asking *you* that. What were you doing in my home?"

He holds up pawed hands. "I was only helping you out."

"You're sure you're not scavenging?"

He cocks his eyebrow at me, which looks comical in his half-formed state. It disconcerts me. We stare at each other.

"Who are you?" I finally ask.

"I'm a deliverer."

"You're—what?"

"I brought you some gloves." He gestures back to the house.

"Gloves?"

"Gloves," he repeats.

"Okay, then," I say. "It's probably time for you to go."

He sighs. "Fine." But he doesn't move.

"Now," I say.

"I'm going, I'm going." He walks away but turns back and says, "Your place was ransacked while you were gone, and I was cleaning up a bit. I got a message from Greyson that your gloves may have been ruined in the rain. He wanted you to have new ones."

"Greyson?" Oh. I remember now. Their clothing-delivery charity. "You're his brother."

"Guilty. Name's Blayde."

"Thank you," I reply, flustered. "Who ransacked my home?"

"Insufferable incarnate." Blayde shakes his head, losing some of his joviality. "They want you to think you don't belong here."

"You're incarnate," I point out.

Blayde grins. "But I'm not insufferable."

I raise my eyebrows, but I can't help smiling at him. "I'm sorry about my reaction."

He shrugs. "Can't say I wouldn't have acted the same if I'd found a wolf in my house."

I eye him. "Why do you stay Suspended?"

He glances down at his half-formed state, then runs his paws through his furry hair that licks his ears in sweet, almost babylike curls. I'm startled to find I'm looking at him fondly, as if he is *my* baby brother.

"I'm cuter this way." He flashes me another grin, and I laugh.

"I think you are the most insufferable incarnate I have ever met. How old are you?"

"How old do I look?"

"How old do you look, or how old do you *act?*" I quip.

He barks out a laugh. "I'm fourteen."

"Awfully young for dangerous missions."

"Eh. The clothes haven't tried to strangle me."

I snort. "Well, now I know my home is safe from incarnate and squatters and little wolf pups, would you like to be invited in for dinner?"

"Thank you, but I must return to my mama." He grimaces, but not, I think, because of his mother. I think it's because he doesn't like being told what to do.

I laugh and am surprised at how often in these few short minutes this kid has elicited that response from me when I originally thought he was there to do—what, I am not sure. "Thank you for the gloves."

"You haven't seen them yet. You might hate them."

"True. If I do, I'll use them as kindling."

"Suit yourself."

"Goodbye, Blayde."

He gives me a ridiculously deep bow. "I'll check in on you again soon."

"When your mama isn't enforcing bedtime?"

He growls. "You wound me." He then forms into his incarnate body, leaps on my chest, and licks my cheek, then barks and takes off at a run.

His departure leaves a chill in its wake, and I shiver. But I put one foot in front of the other, unsaddle Berne, and settle him in the stable with hay. I gather firewood and go back to the cottage, but it's dark now, and the loneliness is heavy and cold.

I light a small fire and eat some food we have in the pantry. How did Greyson get to Blayde, and Blayde get to our place, before I even got home? I remember the gloves and wonder where Blayde placed them. I look around and spy something bulky on the table. Unlike the first pair Greyson gave me, which were black wool, these are made of soft, velvety leather and, as I place them on my hands, I know they're the warmest—and probably most expensive—gloves I've ever owned.

And they're gray.

SIXTEEN

'm still snuggled in my cloak when the sunlight hits my eyelids, and a brown wolf lies at my feet. He lifts his head, opens his maw, and yawns.

"Mama let you leave?"

He tilts his head and barks once.

I scratch behind his ears. "You going to be my guard dog?"

He nuzzles my hand and licks it.

"You know, you're right. You are much cuter as a wolf."

He growls.

"Can't you talk in your wolf form?"

He stretches like the sleepy dog he is, but he keeps stretching and suspends himself between wolf and boy. He shrugs. "No," he says simply.

I wonder why. All the incarnate can communicate telepathically, even to amorphous.

But I know what it's like to be different, so I don't pressure him to talk about it.

"How long have you been here?"

"I went home to Mama, but she told me to turn my tail right back around. 'She's so young, Blayde,'" he says in a high-pitched voice that makes me snort. "'And your brother says she needs watching over.'"

My smile falters. Greyson is spying on me through the eyes of his brother. "Do you and your mother know…?" I pause.

"Why you need watching?" Blayde shakes his head. "He just said you needed to be."

I breathe a sigh of relief. I'm not sure I want to talk about my resurrected sister who is also the heir to the Miadien throne.

"Are you a troublemaker?" Blayde asks, smirking.

I eye him and ignore his question. "How did he get to you, and you get here, before I arrived?"

He grins. "Shortcuts."

I raise an eyebrow, but he just continues grinning. "Fine," I say. "Breakfast?"

"Always."

I fry the few eggs we have left and produce some dried fruit from the depths of the pantry. Trying not to worry about coming up with my next few meals, I enjoy eating this one with Blayde, who burps loudly when he's done and rubs his stomach with one clawed hand, while tousling his unruly brown hair with the other. He grins at my raised eyebrows. He must not understand that I'm waiting for him to excuse his manners because he just says, "Thanks. I'll bring you some bread and cheese later."

"You don't have to do that. I have—"

"You've got hardly anything. Those incarnate pieces of dung—uh, I mean, excuse me, those insufferables, took everything."

"I can go to market this week, and—"

"No, you can't. Once the law is signed into order, you won't be welcome anywhere."

He doesn't meet my eyes, and it's like he's embarrassed that he's an incarnate, that he is somehow responsible for what his kind are doing to mine.

"She's just signing that we can't marry," I say, surprised it sounds like I'm defending the law in any way. Or perhaps I'm trying to convince myself that nothing worse could happen.

"More laws will follow."

I know this. Blayde must know this because of Greyson. How much does he share with his young brother? More to the point, Blayde doesn't seem to care for incarnate or for the law. He and his brother work together to provide food and clothing for those in need, and a great many amorphous are going to need a lot if they are shunned by society.

I don't understand how Greyson can serve the queen and also share the same feelings with his brother. Perhaps their ideas about incarnate and amorphous aren't mirror images, though. I've never heard Greyson talk about the incarnate the way Blayde does. I'm about to ask when Blayde stands.

"I'm going to take a dip in the lake," he says.

"It's probably cold," I point out, "as it *is* autumn."

He shrugs. "I need a bath."

I laugh as he heads out the door. I spend my time cleaning the cottage, straightening up, keeping the fire going since I know Blayde will be cold when he comes in. But then again, maybe not. He's incarnate.

When he returns, I'm curled up in a chair, reading, and he plops down at my feet again. Then, grinning, he hands me a bag.

"What is this?" I ask, taking it from him and opening it. I gasp. "Chocolate? Where did you find this?"

He shrugs. "After I cleaned up, I went into the village. I figured you deserved a treat."

"You didn't have to do that."

"Don't get used to it."

"I won't," I say, laughing, which morphs into a moan the moment the candy hits my tongue. I close my eyes and lean my head back, letting the sweetness fill my mouth. When I open my eyes, Blayde is looking at me, and he hurriedly turns away.

"Here," I say, handing him the second piece that's in the bag, "take it."

"Ah, no, I got it for you," he replies.

"I know," I say, "and I'm sharing with you." I hand him the chocolate, and he grins, then pops it into his mouth.

We sit in silence while the fire flickers, painting the room in shadows and light, until he's snoring. I put a blanket over him and make myself bread and jam, setting aside a piece for him later. I settle back into my chair, wondering if I could just live like this forever. Alone. Undisturbed.

My eyelids flutter. When I'm in the space between dreams and consciousness, I'm jerked awake by a crash accompanied by the tinkling of breaking glass, and then it's all fire. Someone has tossed a torch into the cottage, and the flames are spreading quickly.

Blayde shouts as he jumps up from his place on the floor, and I scream, heading for the door to get a bucket of water, but Blayde grabs my arm. "No! They want to draw you out. You have to let this go. You have to leave!"

I jerk my arm out of his grasp. "This is my home!"

Blayde looks like he wants to say something, but instead, he changes into a wolf and leaps out the window, jaws snapping. I catch the briefest sight of three other warsol—one fox, one coyote, and the other looks like a wolf but in giant-size. An Edge-wolf. I don't know much about Edge-wolves except that they are bred specifically for size and strength, and they are bound to a crowe for life when a crowe forces a collar on them with dark magic.

Blayde is too young, too small to be fighting them. Especially because the fourth person in the party is a crowe. Probably the Edge-wolf's master. I pick up the blazing torch and toss it out the window, then beat the flames with Mama's favorite drapes. But it's too late because the fire is spreading too quickly. I drop the drapes, coughing from the smoke, and grab the cloak Greyson gave me. I'll need it as it gets colder, and soon, the fire will take the walls and roof of my only shelter.

I run outside, but I take the back door, away from where

the warsol are fighting. I could keep running, get away and never come back, but I stop. Berne's still in the stable. I could stay in there, hide. A whine penetrates my ears, followed by a howl of pain, reminding me that Blayde is fighting those monsters for me. The cloak falls from my arms as I run back to the front of the house where the Edge-wolf has its jaws in Blayde's throat.

"Stop!" I scream. Rocks litter the path that leads to my now-burning cottage, and I pick one up, throwing it at the Edge-wolf, but it misses its head where I was aiming and grazes its cheek. It's enough. It loosens its hold on Blayde who, bleeding and whimpering, suspends himself between wolf and boy. He presses his hand to his throat.

"I am Captain Greyson's brother," he says, his voice raspy. "He will hear of this."

The Edge-wolf's eyes flicker between Blayde and me. Then, slowly, it backs away. As it does, it forms back into a human—a girl, not much older than Blayde and me. Blayde's blood drips from her mouth, but tears stream from her luminous eyes, which are round and blue like the moon in winter. Her dark hair resembles the coat of her fur, and she clasps a shaking hand over her mouth.

The other two warsol have formed into humans, too, a woman and a man, although I can't tell which creature they just turned from.

The crowe, a man, laughs and pats Blayde on the head. "It's okay, pup. Faylia here just wanted to play. Come, Faylia."

The Edge-wolf-turned-girl has a steel collar around her neck that looks like a curved feather, and a leash trails to the ground from it.

"Play?" Blayde snarls. "You burned a home and almost killed an innocent girl!"

The crowe raises his feathery eyebrows. "Innocent? And you said you're Captain Greyson's brother?"

Blayde snaps his mouth shut, but he doesn't lower his defiant gaze. While the crowe's eyes are fixed on Blayde, Faylia looks at me, and I want to rush to her and take off that wretched collar. She lowers her gaze.

The crowe chuckles darkly at Blayde's silence, and Faylia brings up her head. She curls her upper lip at her master and explodes into her wolf form again.

Blayde shouts, I scream, and the crowe whirls around. The warsol man lunges for the leash, grasping it in his hands, but she's too strong for him. She drags the warsol man behind her as she runs in circles.

The woman shrieks as Faylia causes the man to crash into her, and they both go down. The man's grip on the leash is tight, but Faylia jerks herself away, snapping the connection between the leash and collar.

The man falls on his back as the tension releases. He curls into a ball, expecting, I think, for Faylia to attack him. But she has already moved away from the warsol and turned her huge form on the crowe. He bares his fangs and swipes at her with his black talons. His wings beat, and he rises a few feet from the ground, but he's not too far out of reach for her. As huge as she is, all she has to do is take one leap, and she has him by his throat. She brings him crashing down, and a sound, that of delicate wing bones breaking, cracks through the air. His fingers claw at her maw, fighting for his life.

I move slowly toward them.

"Anna," Blayde breathes, "no."

I ignore him and hold my hands out to the Edge-wolf. "Faylia?" My voice has a slight tremor to it, but I clear my throat, and when I speak again, it's steady. "I can remove your collar. I just need you to let the crowe go."

The bleeding, broken crowe on the ground widens his eyes as though he thinks I'm doing this to save his life rather than hers.

"Faylia," I say again softly.

Her big eyes go from the ice blue of the Northern Sea to

the turquoise of the seas near Innes Isle. Her jaw relaxes, but she doesn't let go completely.

I'm close to her now, so close I could touch her bristling black fur.

"It's okay," I whisper.

She opens her mouth and drops the crowe like he's a nasty bit of food she didn't mean to eat and settles onto her haunches, lowering her head.

The crowe struggles to his feet, his taloned hand fumbling in his pocket. "You ignorant beast," he growls, and then, there is a flash of silver.

"Stop!" I shout.

He turns, and the dagger meant for Faylia finds itself in my rib because I have pushed her out of the way. I scream and grasp my side, shaking as I pull my hand away from the bleeding wound.

Blayde roars and goes full wolf, ensnaring the crowe's knife hand in his jaws. The ripping of flesh and bone makes me want to vomit, or perhaps it's the pain in my side causing me to be sick. Faylia, still in her wolf form, catches me and places her paw over my wound. The crowe's screams are guttural, but Blayde's returning snarls are ferocious and unforgiving.

The rhythmic pounding of hoofbeats from afar draws my attention to the road that snakes its way from the river to my family's property. Redford leans forward in his saddle, riding as if death is snapping at his heels. His horse slides to a stop, kicking up dust and creating a funnel cloud.

"Anna!" he shouts, climbing from the horse before it has even fully stopped. He takes in my soot-stained hands, the ash falling into my hair, the black charcoal slashed across my face. The blood trickling from my side. The tears streaming down my face. The wolf looming over me.

"Who are you?" he growls at Faylia, who whimpers.

"She didn't do this," I say through clenched teeth. "It was the crowe."

"What crowe?" Redford asks.

We look around. The crowe is gone, along with the warsol, and Blayde sits at the skeleton tree, ears alert, watching the tree line. The outlines of three shapes disappear into the forest.

When Blayde turns, he is partway through changing into his human form, and he looks more like his brother than he ever has before. He wipes the blood from his mouth, then vomits and falls to his knees.

SEVENTEEN

edford situates me in front of him on his horse. My wound is bandaged with the sleeve of his shirt, and I'm wrapped tightly in my red cloak. I fumble in the pockets and breathe a sigh of relief when my fingers brush the leather gray gloves Greyson gave me.

"You have somewhere to go, wolf pup?" Redford asks.

"Yeah," Blayde says.

"Thank you for helping Anna," Redford says. "Both of you."

Faylia bows her head.

Blayde massages his throat. "Yeah, but also, maybe keep your fangs out of my neck?"

A deep rumble comes up her throat, and it sounds like she's laughing. Then, she stretches her neck out far and her legs out in front of her, her rear end going high. She does it again. And again. Then, she lets out a long, piercing howl, and throws her body onto the ground. She growls, but it sounds strangely like she's trying to say something. The incarnate can speak to the amorphous by impressing words in our minds, but Faylia seems unable to do that because she's not able to communicate.

"She can't change," Blayde says, almost in a whisper.

"And she can't speak," I say, my voice as hushed as Blayde's. "Why not?"

The question isn't directed at anyone in particular, but Blayde answers. "I think she's Stranded."

I blink. I've heard of that, but it was only a scary story meant to scare young warsol, something that happened a long time ago. "I didn't think that happened outside the stories."

"I guess it can still happen. Or perhaps," Blayde adds, almost to himself, "the crowes brought it back." He scowls.

"You suspend yourself," I point out.

"By choice," Blayde replies. But he doesn't meet my gaze.

Warsol suspend themselves between forms all the time, but they can always communicate in their minds. Blayde can't. He freely turns wolf when needed, but he never really turns fully human. If being Stranded can happen, then being Suspended might be a condition, too. Maybe some warsol can't change back to humans, so they remain stuck between the two forms. But because incarnate is the majority, the norm, no one mentions it. If warsol can change into an animal—or be part-animal, part-human—then they're incarnate. If they are Stranded, they're simply an animal. And then there's me. Amorphous, not really worth much at all. Too human-like.

"I don't think this is Faylia's choice," Blayde says.

"How was she able to get away from her crowe master?" Redford asks.

"The warsol was holding the leash that was attached to her collar," I say. "And she fought against it, and the leash snapped away from the collar." I struggle to get off the horse, but Redford holds me tightly.

"Where are you going?" he asks.

"Her collar," I say. "I told her I would remove it. If that's all it takes—"

"You can't take it off," Redford says, and I look at Blayde for confirmation.

"It can only be done by the crowe master." He shrugs, and Faylia nuzzles his head. He ruffles the fur on her neck. "I didn't think Edge-wolves could defy their masters, though."

"Will he be able to track her with it on?" I ask.

"There's only one way to find out," Blayde says. "Run. Hide. I'm good at that. And maybe I can ask a crowe if there is any way to take it off other than the master doing it."

"Why would you talk to a crowe?" I ask sharply.

"The crowes are incarnate allies," he says.

"The crowes," Redford says, "are in the service of the queen, but the warsol governance of them is about as secure as a frayed thread. And what's more, that crowe just attacked you."

"I beg to differ," Blayde says. I'm surprised his smart mouth hasn't gotten him into bigger trouble. "They attacked Anna, the amorphous. They only got to me because I was told to protect her."

I don't know why, but this admission smarts. It makes me wonder if he actually cares or is just following orders.

"They are the queen's allies," Redford replies coldly. "She allows those collars to be made. What makes you think a crowe will try to help you get it off?"

"What makes you think they won't?"

Faylia rubs her head against his shoulder. She's so tall, she nearly reaches his full height in her wolf form. It draws a smile out of me, but seeing her Stranded makes me sad. And angry. The amorphous are not the only ones mistreated and subjugated by the incarnate. I'm ashamed of my ignorance, of my fleeting thoughts about the mistreatment of the Edge-wolves. They are so far away from Miadien in the Edges that I haven't considered their plight before.

"We should go," Redford says quietly, putting a hand on my shoulder.

Blayde touches my knee lightly. "I wish we'd met under different circumstances, but since neither of us died, I can say it was a pleasure."

I blink. Just a second ago, I assumed he only protected me because he was asked to. Which, on reflection, is probably true, but that doesn't mean he doesn't care. I smile back, and when our eyes meet, I get the feeling I won't see him again. It makes me ache so much that tears trickle down my cheeks again.

"Thank you, Blayde," I say through the tightness in my throat. "And Faylia. You deserve better than what you've had, and I can assure you, if you travel with Blayde, you'll be with the best."

Blayde rubs the back of his neck. "Shucks, Anna. Making me blush." But he grasps my hand and kisses it. "Be well, Anna of the Foxes."

Redford turns his horse, and we ride toward his home. Berne is tied by a lead to the saddle, and he follows obediently. I glance back, and two wolf shapes prowl away from my now-burned cottage. The small one pauses, lifts his nose to the moon, and howls.

edford knocks quietly on his own front door.

Clary opens it slightly, one blue eye peering at us. When she recognizes us, she opens the door and ushers us in, closing it quickly behind us. "Anna!"

She helps me to the cot next to the fire, which I assume is hers. I sit on the edge, and she helps me struggle out of my cloak. She moves to put it on the ground, but I reach out, unwilling to let it go. I clutch it in my fist. Redford goes into his parents' room, leaving Clary to tend to my wound.

She pulls off my now-crimson shirt. "What plant can help stop the bleeding, Anna?"

I glance at her. "Why are you asking me? You're the one who was in healer training."

She smiles. "Just tell me."

"Yarrow."

"You haven't forgotten, then."

"Not all of it," I say, not meeting her eyes.

"We can use your skills," she says softly as she moves to the medicine cabinet. She pulls out a bottle of the healing balm.

"We?" I ask, raising my eyebrows.

Clary raises hers in turn. "You mean he hasn't told you about the Rising?"

Rebels. Against the crown. Against my sister. "Is that what the rebel group is called? Yes, he did tell me. Partly. I didn't realize you were part of it, too."

"I'm skilled at healing wounds, but I always remembered you being more knowledgeable about the plants themselves. What they do, how to make them into substances we can use."

I shrug, but I wince because the movement made my skin tug on the tear in my side. It's true that studying the plants was always my favorite part. I wasn't particularly excited about seeing blood and gore. "How would my talent for plants and herbs help your group?"

She grins, and the coyote inside her is so visible even in her human form, I nearly pull away. "Poisons are just as effective as bows and arrows."

I stare at her, but she looks away, dipping her fingers into the bottle of balm, then spreads it over my wound. Her touch is light and soft. A healer's touch.

"What about going back to the castle?" I ask. "Repaying your debt?"

Clary swallows. "Perhaps I will when the throne is under another person's rule."

Redford comes out of his parents' room just as Clary finishes pulling a nightdress over me. He's carrying another cot and some blankets. Clary helps him set it up and make the bed, while I sit on her cot, wounded, helpless, grieving. I had a family once. Mother, father, sister. I lost that sister, but Mama and Papi and I had tried. We were treading water when I thought filling my sister's shoes would work, but then

London's reappearance sucked me back under the waves. And now, Mama and Papi have chosen to stay in the castle of the incarnate queen, of the daughter they once lost and have now regained. London might not support a law that forbids the amorphous from marrying, but her solution is to change us by using me to make her potion.

Maybe it's because I'm so tired or feel so betrayed by everyone, that I'm shaking in anger. Potions to force a change, or poisons to kill my enemies. This is what my life has come to.

EIGHTEEN

From beyond the door, the low timbre of Redford's voice travels back to me as he explains to Delilah and Waite what has happened. I curl up in a ball and bury my head under my pillow. I don't want to hear my tragedies retold. They still haven't left the backs of my eyelids, images imprinted in dark shapes as if they have been burned there by the sun's harsh rays. I open my eyes and blink, trying to wipe them away, trying to make myself go to sleep. But I am drowning in decisions I have to make with the few choices available. My family is tucked away nicely in the incarnate castle, my home is burned down, and the only person left who can teach me more about the one thing I'm good at, plants, is here.

I could run. Would the aeobanach take me in? After the skirmish London mentioned, the one that took Greyson's father's life, will they close their borders for fear of being overwhelmed by amorphous warsol? Adderin is under Istreyan law, so that's likely not an option, either. And the Edges... well, there is no way I would be welcome in crowe country.

The only thing I have, really, is Redford. My decision is made for me, my hand forced by my sister and her aunt, the queen.

Clary stirs in her cot and mumbles something in her sleep. I could wake her and confide in her, tell her what occurred at the castle, but I don't want to talk. I don't even want to think anymore. Sleep somehow finds me, although it's turbulent, and I wake to the heavy pre-dawn darkness. The fire hasn't even died down to smoldering coals when I give up on getting any more rest. Small bursts of flame crackle. I stay curled under the blanket, though, because the chill of the morning is trying to slip in between the walls where the chinking has worn thin.

Clary rolls over, and her eyes meet mine. She blinks a few times, making the reflections of the fire in her eyes look like winking stars. The door to the bedroom opens, and Redford treads quietly across the floor.

"I'll do it." The words surprise even me.

Redford stops dead. He must've assumed I was asleep.

But Clary sits up, brushing her curls away from her face, and smiles at me because she knows exactly what I'm talking about.

"I'll be your poison maker."

"Anna?" Redford sinks to the floor beside my cot, eyes questioning. His voice is hoarse from lack of sleep.

"How quickly can we plan a wedding to be sure we're married before the law is signed?"

Redford grasps my hand, kneading the knuckles softly. "Are you sure?"

"Yes," I whisper. "Yes, I'm sure."

The corner of his mouth quirks slightly.

"Are you certain you want to take me on with all of my problems?" I try to make it sound like a joke, but the quaver in my voice betrays me.

The click of the front door closing indicates Clary has left us alone to talk.

"Anna," Redford says, "you are not a problem."

This time, I do laugh. "You misheard me. I said I come with problems, not that I *am* the problem."

He laughs, too, but then his expression becomes serious. "And you want to join the Rising?"

"Yes," I whisper.

He takes my face in his hands and kisses my forehead, hard. "I will get our license today. Mama can help you make a dress. Do you... do you want to send a message to the castle?"

"No," I say, almost before the words are out of his mouth.

"I understand."

Of course he does. He completely understands. He's the only person who does. And that makes him my family, the only member remaining.

"I promise to do everything I can to make you happy." He cradles my face and rubs his thumb along my cheekbone, and I lean into his warmth. He is safety, and since London died—or when I *thought* she died—he is the only one who has given me any spark of happiness.

"I will do the same for you," I reply.

He leans forward, and I'm afraid he's going to kiss me. Oh galaxies above, I will be expected to kiss him soon, won't I. Not that it would be an awful thing. He presses his forehead to mine and inhales through his nose, and the breath is shaky in his chest.

"I do love you, Anna," he whispers.

I love him, too, but I don't respond because a flash of silver eyes and gray hair dances through my mind, and I know I will always wonder what could have been.

"I'll go as soon as the sun comes up," he whispers, then stands as Clary walks back in and Delilah enters the room.

Clary and Delilah begin preparations for breakfast, while Redford goes back into the bedroom to get ready for his short journey. I remain for a few moments sitting on my cot, wondering why this ache in my chest is part pain, part happiness.

NINETEEN

elilah finds some gold material buried deep in her trunk, and Clary comes back from her home, her body changing from a pretty white coyote to her human form as she enters the front yard, with ribbons that have autumn leaves embroidered on them. Her blue dress billows around her as she hurries up the path to Redford's cottage.

"We can sew these to the sleeves and hem of your dress," she explains, "and around your neckline."

"I can honestly just get married in this," I say, gesturing at my attire, trying to ignore the fact that another man gave the clothes to me.

"Psshh," Delilah says and clucks her tongue. "You don't get married in breeches!"

Clary's wild cloud of hair bobs up and down in agreement in the background.

I finger the delicate, brightly colored leaves. "Thank you," is all I can muster around the lump in my throat.

She seems to understand I want to say more because she pats my arm.

"And you, too, Clary. These leaves are beautiful."

"They were my mother's," she says. "She had them on a dress that doesn't fit her anymore, and now we have a reason to use them."

After they take my measurements, Delilah sets to work on the bodice and skirt, while I make breakfast and Clary tends to Waite. Then, Clary and I make the sleeves, and we sew the leaves onto the wrists. She does the hem, while I struggle with the neckline, and Delilah takes a much-needed nap. The strain of the pregnancy is apparent on her face and in the way she moves. I'm embarrassed and feel a little guilty for all the work she's doing just for a ceremony.

But it's a major one, I remind myself.

Redford finally returns home. When he walks through the door, I realize I'd had an ache in my chest all day, and it's because he was gone, and I was worried. I kept myself busy with the dress, but now that he's here, my missing him hits me like a stone. Even I am surprised by the way I rush to him, wrap my arms around his waist, breathe in his familiar scent—no ale this time—and close my eyes with relief.

He hugs me back, then draws away and looks into my eyes. "Are you all right?"

I nod, afraid that if I talk, I'll dislodge the lump in my throat that currently dams the tears.

"You can change your mind if—"

I shake my head emphatically, and he smiles, relief flooding his features.

"All right, darling," he says, and I blink at the pet name. But he continues talking as usual. "I have the license, and the village justice has agreed to marry us. And I also have this." He reaches for a box I hadn't noticed him set down when he came in.

"But I didn't—"

"Just open it," he says.

My fingers shaking slightly, I lift the lid and gasp. A crown, one made of autumn leaves strung together with a gold ribbon, sits inside.

"How did you—"

"Clary may have mentioned the leaves and the color of your gown."

This time, I don't fight the tears. They fall freely, and I simply wrap my arms around Redford again, letting him stroke my hair.

"Thank you," I whisper. I hope he knows I don't mean just for the crown.

I sleep much better tonight than I did the night before. My fingers and back ache from sewing, but I find that the heartache has lessened slightly, has been soothed by this new family I'm creating, where I can just be Anna.

We wake up later than normal as we're all exhausted, and today isn't for working. Today is my wedding day. Delilah and Redford make an enormous brunch, complete with coffee and sugar, which nearly makes me swoon. Sugar, like chocolate, is one of those luxuries that have somehow become scarce in the border villages, in the places where the amorphous population is larger than the incarnate.

Redford and I take our mugs outside, enjoying the crisp autumn morning, marveling at the blue sky that serves as a background to the storm of color the forest is becoming. I wrap my fingers around the warmth of my cup, breathing in the aroma of coffee, leaves, and September air.

Redford clears his throat. "Tonight, after the wedding, maybe we could travel a short way to spend the night alone."

"Okay," I croak, pretending to choke on a sip of coffee.

"There's a lovely little lodge about an hour's ride away."

"Do you know if there'll be vacancy?"

"Yes, I know who owns it, and he always keeps a room for me."

I raise my eyebrows at this, but Redford just smiles.

"For Rising purposes. But it is a nice, cozy room."

"That sounds wonderful," I say, and I mean it. It would be nice to curl up with him, talk with him, be with him.

"Anna!" Delilah's voice rings out in the field. "We need to wash your hair!"

Redford laughs. "So it begins," he says, and I sock him in the arm.

"You should bathe, too, smelly wolf."

He lifts his arm and pretends to sniff his armpit. He wrinkles his nose. "You're not even my wife yet, and you're telling me what to do."

"And I'm right."

He laughs again, throwing an arm around my shoulders and drawing me in close. I grin up at him, and his gaze meets mine. We stop, and he slides his arm from my shoulders to my waist and pulls me in. He leans down, but I meet him halfway and press my lips to his. My—our—first kiss. I wonder why I was worried about this, why I was afraid I wouldn't like it, when it is unlike any sensation I've ever experienced. He only stops kissing me when Clary's shrill voice demands that I get my arse into the house. Laughing, we head through the meadow to the cottage.

TWENTY

Redford taps on the front door. After his bath, he'd been ushered to his parents' room to get dressed, then he was scooted outside with his father to take Waite for a few turns around the meadow to get fresh air. Clary had recruited some people to bring a few flowers and contribute a few dishes for the wedding dinner, and Redford and Waite greeted the guests.

Then, Clary and Delilah attacked me with combs and soaps and even a little bit of color for my face.

"Are you ready?" Redford asks.

I adjust a stray curl that has latched itself onto the crown of leaves, then straighten my skirt. "Come in," I say.

I turn when he opens the door, and his eyes light up. They remind me of the brown leaves of November, the ones that valiantly hold to the branches despite the cold winds and the coming snow. His tunic is gold, like my dress, and his coat is as green as the meadow.

"You...." He stutters to a halt, then clears his throat. "Beautiful."

I lower my eyes, smiling slightly. "You, too, Redford."

"Clary is directing the last few guests to their seats."

I smile. "She's been much more than just a simple healer to your father."

"Like a sister." He blanches. "I'm sorry, Anna, I really shouldn't have—"

I cut him off by waving it away. "It's fine. And you're right. She has acted like a sister. A loyal one." Now I clear my throat because I didn't mean to say it with such an edge.

Or maybe I did.

A lone violin begins to play, our cue that it's time. Redford holds out his elbow, and I place my arm in the crook of it. We glance at each other every few seconds as we leave the little home. I try not to shake as we pause in the doorway, waiting for the village justice to raise her hands and indicate to the guests—there are very few—that the couple has arrived. When all eyes have turned to us, we walk to where the justice waits underneath two aspens that are bowed toward each other.

When we reach her, she nods to the guests to sit and says, "Please face each other and clasp hands."

Redford's are warm and firm, and his grasp makes my hands stop trembling.

"We are here to join two separate lives and make them one," the justice says, "and to forge your spirits together, packmates for life and in the hereafter, should you choose that beyond the eternal gate."

Redford squeezes my hands. I blink fast as the tears start to sting because even though I have this new family, I wish my mother was here to give me an encouraging smile, and that my father was sitting next to her, holding back his own tears.

And my sister. But if London was here, she'd be standing in my place.

"Redford, you have selected Anna of Linden and Belle to be your alpha. Will you choose her every day as your wife?"

"Yes," Redford says without hesitation. "I will."

"Anna, you have selected Redford of Waite and Delilah to be your alpha. Will you choose him every day as your husband?"

"I—" I choke, then swallow hard. "Yes."

The justice claps her hands once.

"Then you, Anna and Redford, are bound. May your life together be blessed and long. Do you have a token you wish to exchange?"

I start to shake my head, but Redford winks at me. He drops my hands and reaches into his pocket. He pulls out a gold ring that is etched with leaves.

I gasp quietly and snap my head up to look into his eyes. "Where... and how?"

He just shakes his head, indicating he'll tell me later, but all that matters now is he's lifting my left hand and sliding the beautiful token of his devotion onto my fourth finger.

"But I don't have anything—"

"I don't need it," Redford replies.

The justice gestures for the guests to rise. "Redford and Anna, you now must sign the scroll." She procures a paison feather quill and a writing board, and we sign our names. She does, too, then says, "You are husband and wife, pack-mates for life, bound by your love, loyalty, and the law as it is written."

The guests clap, and Redford cups my face in his hands. I place my hands on his hips, and he leans in, kissing me softly. I think I know what to expect since our first kiss this morning, but this isn't the same. That one was tentative, sweet, and exploratory. This one claims us as one now, binds us as a couple.

The guests cheer, and Clary lets out a shrill whistle.

We break apart when we hear the long howl of a wolf.

TWENTY-ONE

recognize the young wolf and his gigantic companion immediately. Blayde snarls, and Faylia growls as they make a circle around the wedding party, but they aren't looking at us. Their snouts are pointed toward the tree line. Dark shadows loom under the canopy of the forest. Red pinpricks among the flickering green of night-vision eyes indicate a crowe is among them.

Is it the same crowe who burned down my home, ruined my life? The ring Redford just placed on my finger presses into my skin as I clench my fist.

Not ruined. I have a new family to protect now.

"Anna," Redford says, "get my parents. Take them inside."

"Redford, I—" I press my lips together to stop the words. He's not ordering me to leave. He's not making me go inside because I am weak.

"Please keep her safe," Redford says softly. Then, with his voice raised, he says, "Any other amorphous who choose not to fight, or who can't fight, can shelter in the cottage."

I take Delilah by her hand, helping her into the cottage. Two other women, Delilah's cousin Leigha, and another close neighbor, help Waite into the cottage behind us. I wait for a few moments for others to join us, but no one does, so I shut and bar the door, and we huddle in the middle of the room, far from the windows.

The noise of shuffling feet, moving bodies, and clanking of what few weapons are available sounds around the outside of the cottage. Fast, frantic talking comes directly under the kitchen window, and then I hear a cold voice that sends ice into my veins.

"I have come to inform you," the male voice says, "that this wedding is illegal."

This is not the same crowe who burned my home.

"Phoenix, Queen of Miadien, has signed into law that no amorphous should marry or perform acts of breeding from this day forward."

My limbs tremble like branches shaken by a rough wind, and my gut lurches like I'm being thrown from a horse. Shouts come from beyond the walls of the cottage, protestations that it's unfair, unjust, unlawful.

The cold voice laughs. "I am only enforcing the law. You want to protest it? Take it up with the queen." He pauses. "You. Justice. Where is the marriage scroll?"

"The marriage has not yet been performed," she says.

"Then, you will have no problem handing it over."

Another pause, and Delilah and I glance at each other. I bite my lip. She grimaces. I crawl over to the window to look outside.

"I think you are mistaken," the justice says. "This is a pre-wedding ceremony. I don't have the scroll."

The cold-voiced crowe stands in the center of the group of crowe conspirators. I've never liked the crowe word for soldier, but it does describe their sneaky behavior. The leader's coal-colored feathers meld with the black of the oncoming night, and his eyes, scarlet embers, are like two blood moons hanging in the sky. He smiles, but it's far from pleasant. His lips split as if they have been slashed by a knife.

"I think you are lying," he says. Without looking away from her, he says to a crowe on his right side, "Arrest her."

"No," Redford says, but the justice holds up her hands, both to stop Redford from speaking and to allow herself to be shackled.

"And check her pockets," the crowe continues as the justice's wrists are bound together.

The conspirator binds her roughly and shoves his hands in her pockets, searching, but he comes up empty.

The leader's eyes smolder. His temple bounces, his jaw grinding. "That is the last marriage you will ever perform," he hisses, "legal or not."

"Fine," the justice says. "I don't believe there is anything more for you to do here."

The conspirator who bound her draws out a small club so swiftly, not even those closest to her could have warned her. He hits her upside the head, and she crumples.

I cover my mouth with my hand, trying to prevent the strangled scream that claws its way up my throat from escaping. I drop back down to the floor, breathing rapidly. I don't understand how they found out about our wedding so quickly. The thought of Greyson flashes through my mind, wondering if he's still watching me. But he wouldn't have sent crowes to arrest me. Cold bursts in my stomach, a gut reaction to the idea that Greyson betrayed me because I chose someone else.

A torch crashes through the window, and I'm so exhausted of fire that I let out a scream. "Get out!" I shout, trying to help Waite to his feet, while the other two women carry Delilah out of the cottage and into the dark meadow, away from the fire and the now-ruined wedding.

Waite and I limp to the meadow, where we crouch with Delilah and the others in the tall grass. Delilah screams, a pain that means a new life is ripping its way through hers.

"Clary," I murmur, scanning the area for her bright blonde curls. She's with Redford, who argues with the crowe.

"Help her and stay here," I hiss to Leigha. And then I go head-on into the chaos.

I creep around the blazing cottage and hide behind a few crowe conspirators, who are so focused on their leader that they don't notice me.

"We've come to recruit incarnate to our queen's cause," the leader says. "If you are incarnate and you volunteer, your amorphous friends and relatives will not be harmed."

The uproar at this is deafening. Shouts, screams, even wails. The crowd pushes against each other, and I get caught in the middle between my wedding guests and the gatecrashers. Redford sees me, and his eyes go wide. He fights the crowd to get to me, but it's like fighting against a tidal wave, and I'm being taken farther and farther out to sea.

And then I am shipwrecked, slamming into something. A hard, bony chest. Two black-taloned hands steady me.

"Careful there." Despite the fire burning behind me, his voice is so cold, goosebumps scatter over my arms. "You must be the young bride," he says, holding me at arm's length as if he's a friendly guest coming to congratulate me.

I try to shake free, but his talons dig into my biceps, tiny pricks of blood oozing onto the gold material.

The crowe leans closer. "I know who you are, little amorphous," he whispers, "and I would take you to the princess where you will find much better protection than these"—his eyes sweep over the crowd—"ah, citizens."

I jerk my arms, but it only causes his claws to dig deeper. My arms relax and hang loose, and his claws retract slightly.

"Such a shame to ruin your wedding dress," he says, his whisper like an arctic wind. "How about I make you a deal? A sister—"

But he doesn't get the words out. Instead, he shrieks, his mouth going into a triangle like a beak. His body falls onto me, a red arrow sticking out of his back. I try to roll out from underneath him before we hit the ground, but his heavy weight catches my leg, and we crash to the earth. His scarlet gaze meets mine, and in the moment, he looks young, even timid. Darkly beautiful.

"My—sister—" he says in stuttering syllables.

He looks heartbroken. Just like I am about losing the person I loved the most. I am no healer, but I can tell by the way the arrow sits in his back that it hasn't severed the spine. It's not in very deep, either.

"*Help,*" he croaks.

I hesitate. If I help him, he'll continue serving Phoenix, continue destroying families simply because they are, or they love, amorphous. But why do the crowes serve her? They are ruled by Skoll, but they aren't even really free.

"Anna," he whispers, his chest heaving.

I can do one of two things—pull the arrow out or push it deeper in. I grasp the end of it. "What's your name?"

He's losing a lot of blood, and the skin on his face clings to the bones, but his eyes meet mine. "Saffron," he whispers. He reaches out, and I place my hand in his trembling palm.

"Surrender!" Redford shouts. "Surrender now!"

I whip around, wondering if he's demanding that our attackers surrender or if—

No. He's telling *us* to surrender. He's telling us to run. His eyes meet mine. Our wedding guests are either on the ground or running away, and Redford's home is falling down, blackened wood crashing into heaps on the ground. Blayde and Faylia are nowhere to be seen, and my heart contracts. Saying a quick prayer to the galaxies, I close my eyes and remember Blayde's sweet face that clings to the edges of childhood. But he is no child, and I hope he's safe somewhere to grow into a man. I loosen my grip on Saffron's hand and struggle to my feet.

"Please…." Saffron whispers. "Please."

"You will never attack me or hurt me again," I hiss.

Saffron brings his head up. "I will remember."

"Or the ones I love."

He's on all fours, his black wings splayed behind him. "Does that include your sister?"

His question throws me. "You serve my sister."

He cocks his head, and we stare at each other for a few long seconds. "It's complicated."

"It is," I agree. In one swift movement, I rip the arrow from his back and toss it next to him. "Leave my sister to me."

Saffron bows his head. "I will not kill her," he says, but then he starts coughing, and I don't linger anymore.

I run to Redford.

TWENTY-TWO

Iget to him just as he lifts Delilah into his arms.

"Redford," I gasp.

"Get the horses."

I rush back toward the stables, but I veer to the right and go into the burning cottage. An irrational need to retrieve my red cloak seizes me, and I pray to the moon that it hasn't been burned yet. I reach under my cot and pull it out, sighing in relief. I throw it over my shoulders and race to the stables, where I halter Berne, Redford's horse, and the two plow horses that belong to Waite. As I'm leading them out of the stables, a crowe flies into my path. She holds a knife in one hand and a torch in the other. She grins at me as if we're old friends meeting for a drink. I have no weapons, but I do have plow horses. Their lead ropes fall free, and I smack their backsides, startling them into a frantic run. The crowe flaps her wings to lift herself out of the way, but she's not quick enough, and the first horse clips her taloned feet, knocking her sideways in the air. The second, bigger horse smashes into her wing, causing her to crash to the ground. The knife flies from her hand, and she flings the torch away to avoid being burned. Sparks fly, scattering over her face, and she throws an arm over her eyes, screaming. Then, she goes silent. She lies there, unconscious or dead, I'm not sure.

I lead Berne and Redford's horse out. A cold chuckle reaches my ears as I leave. Saffron stands there as if he was waiting for me, holding his chest, looking down at his fallen compatriot.

"I may have made a mistake," he says, holding back a cough. "You're going to be hard to kill since I made a promise not to be the one to do it. My crowes do not appear to be up to the task."

I shrug as though we've had had a friendly disagreement. "That's your problem."

He coughs again, sinking to his knees, but still grinning. "Until we meet again, Anna."

I don't spare him another thought. The horses trot behind me as I run to Redford.

"Hold their leads," he says, then situates Delilah on the back of his horse and helps Clary on behind her. Delilah whimpers, the labor pains still plaguing her.

"Anna will lead," he says to Clary. "Just help her stay on."

I climb onto Berne, and then Redford helps Leigha on behind me.

I look around for Waite. He and the other woman who was with us are nowhere to be seen. "Where's your father?"

Redford meets my eyes and shakes his head. He hands me the other horse's lead rope and transforms into his wolf form. He doesn't look back as he leads us away from the ruins of his home.

"Clary?" I ask, looking over my shoulder.

"His heart failed trying to help his wife not die."

Tears sting my eyes, and I let them fall because Waite deserves my tears.

We ride into the darkness on an invisible path, but Redford, in his wolf form, walks purposely forward. The horses stumble every now and then over branches and roots, but Berne trusts me on his back, so he continues putting one hoof in front of the other. The crown of leaves hangs on the back of my head, secured only by a few locks of my hair. My gown has blood splattered on it, and there are several rips in the skirt. A fissure erupts down the center of my heart at the sight. Like the dress, I'd built my family in one day, and it only took one evening to tear it apart. But my red cloak is safe, and it's keeping me warm in the chilly night and in the freezing terror of all that has passed in only a few short hours.

After about an hour, we enter a clearing where a lodge sits dimly lit. Shadows move behind the windows, their movements barely perceptible. Redford told me there was going to be a room for us at this lodge. But it was meant to be for us to celebrate our wedding. Now, it's a refuge.

Redford transforms and helps his mother and Clary down, rushing them inside, trusting, I think, that I will take care of the horses. Leigha runs inside after them, and I'm alone in the murky clearing, the breathing of the horses the only sound to comfort me. I rest my head on Berne's neck.

The stables are behind the lodge, tucked neatly into a smaller copse of trees. Berne is a gentle soul, so I know he'll be fine sharing a stall with Redford's horse. After I remove their halters, I give them a quick rubdown and then go to the lodge. As soon as I open the door, a scream rakes through the entire building, sending the few occupants scrambling for weapons or, in the case of a young boy, a hiding place.

A long cry and small whimper, that of a newborn baby, floats down the stairs, and I slam the door behind me, running toward the sound, taking the steps two at a time.

A door on the right bangs open, and Redford reaches for me.

I wrap my arms around his neck. "Are they okay?"

"Baby Rowan is fine, but Mama is bleeding too much."

Clary pushes by us, shouting something about towels and needing cranesbill. My stomach drops. The cranesbill herb helps stop internal bleeding. If internal bleeding isn't stopped… I pull back and look in Redford's eyes. He cannot lose both his parents on the same night.

"Go be with her. I'll help Clary find the herbs." I kiss him quickly. "Oh," I say as I'm turning away, "is it a boy or a girl?"

Redford grins. "A boy."

lary bangs around in the kitchen, muttering about useless spices and the need for an herbalist in the Rising. "Damn!" she says as I sit down. I'm still in my wedding dress, and it feels strange to be sitting in the kitchen in it.

"What?"

"I have a small amount of witch hazel. It won't be enough to slow her bleeding. No cranesbill, and it's so late in the season. We need something else."

"Did you harvest any Lady's mantle this year?" I ask, remembering the herb I used to make a tea with for London during her monthly cycle. It, also, is too late in the season to harvest, but if she pulled some at their full bloom and dried them, we could use it.

"Yes!" Clary snaps her fingers but then drops her hand. "But it's not here."

"Did you leave it at Redford's or at your home?"

"My home is probably burned to the ground now, too."

"Oh, Clary. Your family—"

"I sent them to Istreya a while ago," she says, waving it away. "But the other villagers, whether they oppose the law or not, probably got caught up in the crossfire."

We stand in that awful silence, wondering about the fate of our friends and neighbors.

"I can go back," I say quietly. "I'll find the Lady's mantle."

"Redford will never let you go," Clary replies immediately, almost before I even get my suggestion out.

I huff. "We're married, but he's not in charge of me."

Clary rolls her eyes, but she's smiling. "Because he loves you."

I clear my throat.

"Go take off the dress," Clary says. "I have spare clothes in my room."

"I will later. Thank you. Listen, Clary, I know what the herbs look like, and I can—I'm able to not be seen if I don't want to be."

"How's that?" Clary's eyebrows shoot into her hairline.

"I don't really understand it, but when I try to hide, I somehow become, I don't know, invisible." Perhaps that's not quite accurate, but it's the best way I can describe how I'm able to avoid detection.

Clary watches me for a moment, tapping one slender finger to her lips. "You know, Skoll once said magic is like any other talent, one we can choose to hone or not, and one we can choose to manifest in different ways. I thought your magic was with plants."

"It was," I admit, "but then I suppose because I was trying to hide from the world after everything, I just became good at hiding."

"That skill could be useful to the Rising."

"Then let me prove my skill and get the herb before we lose Delilah."

"I kept my stores in the stables. Just be careful." She hands me a water skin. "There is dried fruit and nuts, too, and some cheese you can take."

"What's this?" A man, not much older than Redford, is shadowed in the doorway, his hands on his hips. His eyes are that of an amorphous, crescents like mine. Although there does seem to be something rather wolfish in the look on his face.

He looks from Clary to me and back again. "You're back."

"Yes," Clary says, "both Redford and I are here."

"I understand the mother might not make it."

"We don't have the herbs we need to help her," Clary says. "This is Anna, Redford's wife."

I blink, startled at the new title I bear.

"Anna, this is Zultan."

Zultan's clear blue eyes, so light they are almost white, focus on me. I've seen him before. He's the man Redford was talking to at the inn, the one who he had argued with. Redford had called him his captain. So, this is the leader of the Rising. "And who do you belong to?"

"I—"

"Her father raised her in the capital," Clary says, talking over me. "Single father. He was drafted."

"I see," Zultan says. "What kind of herbs do you need?"

"Lady's mantle," Clary replies, "and Anna has offered to get it."

"And are you committing yourself to the cause, too?"

I look at Clary.

"He means," she explains, "if you are going to stay here, you'll need to become a member of the Rising and perform missions for us."

Zultan's stare is cold as he waits for me to answer.

"She and Redford have just been married," Clary says, "amorphous to incarnate, and I'm sure someone told you about the attack at the wedding."

Zultan scowls. "No one has told me anything about that."

"Sit," Clary says, gesturing to a chair at the table. "I'll tell you everything. Does Anna have your leave to get the herbs? We have none here, and of course there are no fresh herbs this late in the season."

Zultan studies me, and I try not to show my nerves by fidgeting. Finally, he nods, and Clary takes me to the door.

"He'll want an answer to his request that you officially join the Rising," she says. "Just be prepared. And be careful."

In Clary's room, I gather only essentials—a change of stockings in case mine get wet, a blanket, and a spare dress. In the room I'm supposed to share with Redford, I take off my ruined wedding gown and place it in a drawer, where I hope it will remain safe. I slip on Clary's dress, and it fits surprisingly well. My red cloak is the last thing I put on. I slip my hands in the pockets, and my fingers brush something soft. I pull out the gray leather gloves. Tears sting my eyes, and a stone settles in the pit of my stomach. I rush out of my room, hoping if I hurry, I'll somehow keep the tears from falling.

I hesitate briefly by Delilah's door. Letting Redford know I'm leaving will take more time, and he'll try to stop me or insist that he come along. He needs to stay with his mother since he just lost his father. I'm the only one who can retrieve the herb we need to make sure baby Rowan will have his mother to raise him since his father is gone.

Berne is exhausted, and I don't have the heart to ask him for more, so rather than going to the stables, I leave the lodge, slipping between the thick trees to follow near the trail but not on it. I, too, am exhausted. But for Delilah, Rowan, and Redford, I push myself through each step.

TWENTY-THREE

y legs become rooted like the trees, and I try to rip them out of the ground with every step. Running on zero sleep has never been something I could manage. But I push. And push more. And drag myself forward until I trip and land on my hands and knees.

"Fine," I mutter. "Ten minutes." Delilah won't get the herb that will save her life if I die from exhaustion before I can bring it to her.

I find a pine with long, thick branches that curve downward, covering the base of a tree like a skirt. Ten minutes, I think, breathing heavily. I lean against the trunk, pulling my knees into my chest with my hood down and the cloak wrapped around me.

I jerk awake to the fluttering of wings in the trees. Heart pounding, I slow my breathing and shake the sleep fog from my mind. It's way past dawn, according to the way the sunlight slants through the forest—and even past late morning. I curse myself for sleeping so long—for sleeping at all, really. I should have kept going. Luckily, I don't have to pack my things, but as I set to move out, the crunch of fallen twigs and leaves tells me someone is coming close, most likely in their animal form because of the way the footfalls land softer on the ground than booted feet would. I burrow in my cloak, leaving a small opening to peer through.

A giant wolf comes into view, but it doesn't look like it's searching for anything. Rather, it looks like it's trying to avoid being seen, too.

It stops in the path close to my tree, lifts its snout, and inhales. It can probably smell me, but I hope it can't see me. When it turns its face toward me, I see this isn't just any giant wolf. It's an Edge-wolf, and I know her.

Faylia.

The last time I saw her, she was with Blayde. I wonder how and when they got separated, if they chose to part ways. I hope this doesn't mean he has been killed. Blackest skies above, I will kill the crowe who laid a talon on him.

She sniffs again and pokes her nose through the branches. I remain still, wondering if my desire to remain unseen will protect me.

She growls again, and this time, it sounds like a name. *My* name.

Slowly, I lower my hood and crawl toward her. I hold out my hand close to her muzzle, and she pushes her nose into my palm. Her blue wolf eyes find mine as I release whatever magic makes me seem invisible.

"Come in here," I whisper. She wriggles between the branches, looking like a puppy snuggling in for warmth. "Are you all right?"

She whimpers softly. I run my hands over her fur, looking for injury. Thankfully, there are no wounds.

"Where's Blayde?" I ask, and this time, she goes down on all fours, covering her face with her paws. "What is it? He didn't—he's not—"

She looks up at me and growls out what sounds like "no."

"Did he leave you?"

She shakes her huge wolf head.

"Then, why aren't you—" I stop myself. She has no way to answer. Blayde wouldn't have abandoned her, so all I can assume is that they got separated. Not killed. "Were you looking for him?"

She bobs her great head up and down.

"He must be sick with worry for losing you,"

She lays her head on her front paws. The fur on the back of her neck spreads apart so the collar she wears is visible.

"I could still try to remove it," I say. "But I'm afraid of what might happen. Would it tighten around your throat since I'm not a crowe?"

She just stares at me with those clear eyes, and it hits me that we are in similar situations. She is Stranded in her animal form, and I am Stranded in my human form. I stroke her glossy black fur.

"You can stay with me. I need to get back to my village to get an herb to save my mother-in-law's life. She had her pup, but her life is still in danger."

Faylia struggles to her feet and leaves the protection of the branches. She looks back at me expectantly, so I crawl out. She goes down on all fours and stares at me. She growls, and it sounds like she says, "On."

"What? You mean ride on your back? Faylia, no, I can walk." Although, Edge-wolves are known for their speed, which would make this grueling trip a lot faster and easier. She barks, making me jump, then laugh. "All right."

I pull myself onto her back, wincing as I tug on her fur, but she doesn't seem to notice. Just as I'm wondering how I'm going to hang on, she leans her neck down, revealing the collar again. The leather is warm from her body, and I wrap my hands around it, both for the heat and to keep myself on her back. She takes in a deep breath and runs on the exhale.

he smoke drifts from the circle of cottages that surround the villages. Not just Redford's is gone. Several more are, too. I pray to the stars that Clary's stables haven't been razed.

It's later than I wanted it to be, but that's not Faylia's fault. It's mine for sleeping. But if I hadn't stopped, maybe we wouldn't have found each other. We stop at the edge of the woods that enclose the village, scouting for anyone who might be remaining, friend or foe. Warsol move around in the town proper, and smoke from chimneys rather than burned cottages goes up in single gray curls instead of black plumes into the sky. I slide off Faylia's back, belatedly thinking I should have done it sooner, but I keep my arm resting on her body.

"I'm going to Clary's stables. That's where she said the herbs are kept. I can remain unseen—"

Faylia gives a noise that sounds like she's saying, "Hmm?" It makes me laugh.

"It's a trick I've been honing," I tell her, "and I'll explain more later. You stay here, okay?"

She whimpers as I stroke her fur and then leave, pulling up my hood. Clary's family home should have been standing near Redford's, but it's gone, and I avoid looking at where Redford's now sits smoldering. The tree line where we were married is scorched, so I avoid that, too. The stables are blessedly still there, although one wall is burned and close to collapsing. I slip inside, noting all the animals are gone. The soldiers must not be punished for thievery. I head into the tack room. Saddles, bridles, and lead ropes are all gone. The shelves are bare, and there are no visible cabinets. Where else would she keep the herbs? I glance up to check if there are any drying from the ceiling, but if there had been any before, they are gone now.

Maybe they, too, have been taken, and my journey here is a worthless endeavor. No, I correct myself, not worthless. I'm practicing my disappearing skills, and I found Faylia.

But none of that will save Delilah. She could be gone already.

I have bought herbs from the stand in the village before, but I don't have any coin now. I suppose if the royal soldiers can steal without repercussion, I can, too. I spy one old saddlebag hanging limply on a nail and, figuring I'll need something to pack the stolen goods in, I grab it and make my way to the town square, trying to stay on the edges of the village as much as I can. The herb stand is shuttered, but that makes it easier for me to get what I need. I won't have to talk to anyone. Few people roam the streets, and those who do look drawn, scared, and tired. A few, however, seem to be gloating.

Orange light shines from the pub's grimy windows even though it's daytime, and the noise that spills out its open door tells me a celebration is happening inside. Drunken singing and shouting stream into the streets, and inside, the grunts and jeers of warsol echo from the room. They are competing for who is fastest, biggest, worthiest.

No one notices me as I go to the stand and slip inside. The shelves under the counter are lined with herbs and plants, some already harvested into balms, salves, and medicines. Grinning, I shove as many things as I can into the saddlebag. When I'm done, I leave out the back like I own the place, but I've forgotten to hide myself, and I walk straight into a murder of crowes.

TWENTY-FOUR

"Where did you come from?"

The crowe on my right jumped back when I fell into their circle, and now he's staring at me in bewilderment. They are up early, night stalkers awake at midday. Some look exhausted, while others look drunk.

"What do you mean?" I try to sound as innocent as possible. "I'm simply walking." I hope their tired and drunk states will help me pass, but I make the mistake of clutching the saddlebag tighter, holding it to my chest a little closer.

The crowe raises his feathery eyebrows.

The others are now looking at me curiously, but one has his back to me. Slowly, he turns, and our eyes meet.

Saffron.

"Stand down, conspirator," he orders. "Where are you going?" he asks me.

"Home," I reply.

"Then get to it," Saffron says, waving his taloned hand as if I'm a fly buzzing around his face.

I don't look back, but I also try not to run, so I'm close enough to hear the crowe say, "That was an amorphous."

"Obviously," Saffron croaks.

"Why did you let her go?"

"Are you questioning me, conspirator?"

"No, I'm just—"

"Our orders are to stop any weddings between amorphous and incarnate and push the amorphous to the Edges, not kill every single one of them." This is a new voice. "It must come from the princess, not the queen."

"The princess is the voice of the queen," Saffron snaps, "and we must obey if we are to stay in the queen's good graces."

"So, she can dismiss the Crescent," the first crowe responds, "and allow your mother her rightful place as princess of our people. But I—" The crowe is cut off by his own shriek.

I run. Faylia is practically howling by the time I get to her. I throw my arms around her, then look back at the crowes. The one who questioned Saffron holds his face in his taloned hands, and Saffron is wiping off his own claws, staring in the direction I ran.

"Did he just claw his own conspirator?" I whisper, but I don't need her confirmation. The blood streaming through the conspirator's fingers tells me everything. It makes my stomach twist, but my mind whirls with questions. They believe that Saffron's mother should be named the Princess of the Edges, that the Crescent should be dismissed from the Edges so they can rule themselves. The queen's hold on them must be looser than she thinks.

Faylia nuzzles me, jerking me out of my thoughts.

"Yes," I agree to her soft whines, "it's time to go."

I guide Faylia through the trees to the lodge. Candle-light flickers from only a few windows. I climb off Faylia's back, stroking her thick black fur. The stables are lit with the gray light of dusk, dust swirling among the flying insects that buzz around. Faylia doesn't belong in there with the other animals. She's warsol, regardless of her current state.

"Come with me," I say, pulling on her collar. "You can stay in my room."

I had told her about my recent marriage, but I hadn't revealed that my husband is my sister's ex-fiancé, or that she is the princess of the warsol. By the look in Faylia's blue eyes, though, I think she suspects I'm not just another rebel. She pads quietly behind me as I go to the front door, but it won't open. Scowling, I push my shoulder against it and try to force it, but it won't budge.

"What in the dying stars?" I mutter. Faylia's snout points upward as she surveys the lodge and the surroundings. "I hear talking," I say, "so they must be in for the night. They've got to have a back entrance, right?"

Faylia cocks her head, and my mouth quirks up as I imagine her shrugging.

"Come on," I say, leading her away from the front and around the back. Shadows dance behind the lodge's curtains, silhouettes casting gray smudges across the glass panes. We round the corner, and I collide with a solid wall that smells like ale.

"Redford! What are you doing—why are you out here, and why is the front door—"

"Shhh," he says as he waves his hand and peers blearily at me. "Where have you been?"

"Didn't Clary tell you?"

He stumbles backward, catching himself against the wall. Grinning, he brings up a bottle and takes a swig.

I want to slap it out of his hand, but it's none of my business. Wait. Yes, it is. We are bound together now. So, instead of getting angry, I stroke my hand up his arm and grasp the bottle, pulling it away from his mouth. "You don't need this anymore," I whisper. "You have me."

He blinks as if just now seeing me. His head drops to my shoulder, his arms around my waist. "I'm sorry, Anna."

I hold him for a moment, then he yelps and practically throws me behind him.

"What in the deepest blackhole is that?"

Faylia growls, baring her teeth, her eyes sparkling like sapphires against the smoke-colored evening.

"Redford," I say placatingly, "shh. She's... mine."

"That's an Edge-wolf," he says. "Wait a minute." Understanding brightens his eyes. "That's the girl who almost killed that pup."

"Not exactly how that all happened, but in essence, yes. She's going to stay with me. She helped me get this." I hold up the saddlebag full of herbs. "Where's Clary? I need her help to make a tea with this for your mother."

Redford doesn't reply, and I glance at him, then to the bottle, and gasp. "Is your mother—is that why you're out here—"

"She's holding on. This is for my father."

It hurts like a punch to the gut, and the air even escapes my lungs. How could I have forgotten? He lost his father. He has every right to drown his sorrow.

But he doesn't. He dumps the rest of the liquid onto the ground, then takes my hand and leads me into the lodge through a back door, Faylia following closely behind.

"Come on," he says, pulling me through the kitchen. "The door is locked because they are having a meeting in the cellars. I was rather unhelpful."

"Who's with Delilah?"

"Leigha. And me. But Mama was asleep, so I sent Leigha to her room, and then Mama and Rowan fell asleep, too, so I figured I'd step out." He gestures around with the bottle. His eyes are unfocused, and he peeks out the window, squinting up at the sliver of moon that can be seen through the trees.

I frown. That does not sound like the Redford I have known all these years. He would never leave someone he loved who was ill unattended. My eyes stray to the now-empty bottle, and a rush of regrets crashes into me. When he went to the pubs, I should have sought him out, brought him back to my home. I shouldn't have hidden away from the world, from him, because even though I had lost someone, I still had others. My defense against the hurt became a talent for hiding, but it hurt him, and it probably hurt my parents, too, while I unwillingly honed it. And Redford's defense from the pain is from an outside influence that will only drown him.

Faylia brushes against my legs as she sniffs, following a scent up the stairs.

"Faylia?"

She stops and looks at me, cocking her head as if to say, "Well? Come on."

"Okay, okay. I'm coming." This time, I take Redford's hand and bring him with me. Faylia takes us right to Delilah's door. Rowan's cry startles me into pushing the door open without knocking.

Delilah looks like death, but her chest is rising and falling. The baby sleeps in a cradle next to the bed. I pick him up gently, and my heart constricts at his squished little face, his tiny, pursed lips, and little round cheeks.

Faylia's warm body presses against my legs, steady and reassuring that she's here for me. She sniffs little Rowan, and I swear she wrinkles her wolfish nose.

"Yeah," I say, "he needs a change." I look to his brother. Redford sits slumped in a chair, but he hasn't passed out. "Redford, go get Clary. Give her this." I hand him the bag. "Lady's mantle is in there. She'll need to make a tea."

He stands, drawing me to him. He presses his face to my hair. "I'm sorry, Anna," he says again.

"I know. We'll work on it, okay? Just get Clary."

He kisses my cheek and leaves, and I hold out the squirming baby to Faylia. "You want to save me from this little explosion of... well."

Faylia tilts her head to the side. "Mmrp?"

I laugh. "Fine." Rowan squawks as I unwrap him from his

fur blankets, and I nearly make the same noise as I pull off his linen wrap. "Faylia, sniff out where the clean ones are."

Faylia pads around the room, locating a pile of clean wrappings. I've never actually changed a baby's wrap before, but I do my best. His little fist waves sporadically as I wash him off, place the wrap, and then swaddle him back into his fur. I kiss his chubby cheek and put him back in his cradle just as Clary comes in with a tea.

"Anna, you've worked a miracle," she says. "Help me sit her up. What in the blackhole is an Edge-wolf doing in here?" Her words spill out in one long gasp, and I answer her as we wake Delilah and help her to sip the tea.

By then, Rowan is crying for milk, so poor Delilah has to feed him. I help her hold him while he nurses so she can lay her head back.

"Redford," she whispers. "Rowan belongs to him if I…."

Clary, who is busy changing Delilah's sheets, catches my eye. "We're going to send you to Adderin," she says to Delilah softly. "You and Rowan and Leigha. We have a contact there named Rain who, with a group of other aeobanach and paison, are taking in a select number of warsol refugees. I will take you there."

TWENTY-FIVE

My time is split between helping Delilah at night and meeting other members of the Rising during the day. This afternoon, the sky outside is gray and heavy with clouds. It looks like I feel inside, having just sworn my allegiance to the Rising as Zultan requested.

A fire blazes in the fireplace, and both Delilah and Rowan are sleeping. I finish mixing a medicine for Delilah when the clouds open and the rain bursts out in sheets. The sound makes me jump, and I accidentally bang my leg against the night table, knocking over a glass of water.

"Blackhole," I curse, trying to clean up the mess.

"You all right?" Delilah asks, her voice hoarse from disuse.

"Oh," I gasp, "I'm so sorry. I didn't mean to wake you."

"It's no matter," she replies. She glances at the medicine I'm holding in my left hand, while I continue to mop up water with my right. "Is that for me?"

"Yes. Here, I'll help you drink it." She struggles to sit partway up, and I'm able to fluff the pillows behind her. I tip the glass, pouring the medicine in. Some dribbles on her chin, and she wipes it away, giving a small laugh.

"I've never felt so helpless before," she says. "Who knew I'd feel like death when I've just given life?"

I hand her a napkin to clean the rest of her chin and the back of her hand. "It's like you've given part of your own life to him," I remark, looking at baby Rowan. His lips are pursed as he sleeps.

"I do believe that's part of it," Delilah replies, settling back into her pillows. "We do anything for our children."

I place the glass that held the medicine on the night table and keep my gaze outside on the pouring rain. Her words have cut me, although I know she didn't mean for them to.

"It's what your mother has always done for London," she says, and I change my mind and think she *is* saying them to hurt. I turn around, ready to be angry, but find I can't when she looks so pale and drawn. She's speaking in past tense. She doesn't know of this new hurt, this new betrayal.

"I know a little of Belle's story," Delilah says. "I knew her when she arrived in our village, pregnant with London and newly married to your father. And fresh from battle."

"Did she actually confide in you?"

"It took several years," Delilah admits, "but there were times when she'd have too much wine and tell me things." She chuckles. "I know about her past relationship with Phoenix, that she wanted to protect London from ever being found by the queen."

"So, you know she isn't our father's biological child."

"I discovered it in time," Delilah says. "I helped your mother keep the information as quiet as possible. But Anna, my darling, she loves you just as much as she loves London."

"Did you know Falcon?"

"No," Delilah replies softly. "He had already passed away when I met your mother."

"Did he die in battle?"

Delilah considers me for a moment. "Of a sort."

"What does that mean?"

"I don't know everything, Anna, and I especially don't know your mother's emotional state and what was at stake when it happened."

It takes a few seconds for the words to sink in. "Are you saying that *she* did it? She killed her own husband?"

"I don't think the incident was as black and white as that," Delilah says carefully, but I'm already seeing red, and I'm trying hard not to let my thoughts wander dark paths, like the one leading me to think my mother is no better than Phoenix.

"Will you be okay if I take a walk?" I ask abruptly.

Delilah glances out the window at the storm. She must decide it is no match for the one that rages inside of me. "Yes," she replies. "Leigha should be here soon, anyway." I am about to close the door behind me when she says, "Don't judge her too harshly, Anna."

I have to bite back my response because it is not Delilah who I am mad at. It's not Delilah who has lied all these years, who was in the service of the evil princess and married, then apparently killed, the prince. And now she's back in that castle with Queen Phoenix again, serving my sister, and I—I am alone. But I suppose that was my choice.

TWENTY-SIX

The storm beats me back from the door, and I decide what I need is simply a moment to think. I'm nursing a huge mug of coffee when Zultan marches into the common area that also serves as the dining room of the lodge.

"Well, guess how Queen Phoenix celebrated her amorphous-can't-marry law?" he barks.

I don't want to know, but I do want to know.

"She finally introduced the kingdom to her heir."

"Who is it?" Clary asks, who has just come in from the kitchens with a steaming mug, but I already know, so I begin to make my way out of the common area.

"Her niece. Apparently, Prince Falcon had a child before he died, and Phoenix has been keeping her hushed up in the castle ever since."

I stop.

"Princess London of the Warsol, although they may as well change their name to be the incarnate."

I agree silently, but I don't want to hear anymore. I try to slip away, but Clary steps in front of me.

"London?"

I look into her eyes. "Some coincidence," I mutter, but she doesn't let me off that easily.

"Is that what you were summoned to the castle for?"

"Yes."

"But she's dead."

I wince. "That was the argument I kept making, too. But Phoenix's crowes seem to know no bounds when it comes to dark magic."

"He never told me."

"Redford?"

Clary blinks. "No. Skoll."

"Why would he tell you?"

She doesn't answer because Zultan is yelling again.

"But you know what else? We also get a prince."

My heart stutters to a near-halt.

"Who?" shouts an older warsol, whose grizzled face holds the pinched look of a hungry coyote.

"Captain Greyson."

My stomach clenches as though I'm going to be sick.

Zultan laughs bitterly. "So, she announces she has an heir, then, to rub salt in the wounds of the amorphous, she has commanded that her niece marry the captain of her guard. The finest and strongest incarnate match in the kingdom."

Tears sting my eyes, which is ridiculous. Greyson was not mine, never *could* be mine. He doesn't love her. He's being forced to marry her, and—

I am married. I chose to marry Redford.

So, none of this matters.

I spin on my heel and flee the common area, even escaping the lodge as I burst out the door to the now-subsiding storm, pulling in deep gasps. A cold damp nose pushes against my palm, startling me. "Oh! Faylia." I sink to the wet ground and wrap my arms around her neck, burying my face in her soft, black fur.

She makes a humming sound, almost like a cats purr.

"It's nothing," I say as I pull away, wiping tears from my cheeks. "It's ridiculous. I'm married, and so Greyson can get married, but I think—oh, Faylia, I think I may have loved him, loved him from the moment I saw him, like in a story, and now I'll never—" I hiccup. "Not that I could have ever told him anyway."

Faylia lays her great black head in my lap, and I stroke her fur. "I am ridiculous."

"You loved him?"

I gasp, startling Faylia out of my lap, and she jumps up on all fours and growls at the intruder. But he is no intruder. It's Redford, and he looks angry and hurt and lost and confused all at once, a tornado of emotions. I swallow hard and stand, brushing off my skirt and cloak, then rub the mud I've just gathered on my palms back into my pants. "You loved someone else, too, before us."

The anger slides off Redford's face like ice melting in the sun. The hurt remains, though, but he nods. "I'll be going with Clary to take my mother and Rowan to Adderin."

I blink. "You're going to leave me here?"

"It'll be safer."

"But Clary—"

"Is a fighter and a healer. I need to take someone who can handle herself if need be."

That stings, and I try not to flinch. *I can hide, though,* I argue in my mind.

"Besides, Zultan wants you to start experimenting with poisons to put in streams where incarnate and crowes camp."

Before I can say anything, Redford leaves. Faylia looks up at me with her clear eyes, and my own wretched reflection stares back at me.

"I love him, too," I say.

lary finds me in the kitchen, poring over the books and scrolls she lent me. She's been spending much of her free time teaching me from these texts, helping me understand the recipes, the alchemy, and the magic of plants and herbs. It's fascinating, and there were times I was so enthralled with my reading, I'd forget my sister was the traitorous princess of this kingdom, my parents chose her, that I love the man I married but am dying inside because Greyson is marrying London.

Faylia stays by my side at all times. She, rather than Redford, sleeps in my bed with me, while he sleeps in his mother's room to give Leigha breaks. Maybe when this war is over, he and I can find a way to be husband and wife rather than two warsol joined together out of necessity.

"I love him, too," I keep repeating, not to convince myself but to remind myself that my love for him, and his for me, should one day ease all the hurts we've experienced.

"We're leaving today," Clary says. "I'm not sure how long it will take. A few weeks, maybe?"

"Okay." I tap the scroll I've been reading. "I think it's dangerous to poison the streams. What if unsuspecting children get into it?"

"If they're the children of the incarnate, does it matter?"

She's incarnate. So are Redford and Delilah, and baby Rowan is the child of incarnate. What if he stumbled upon a poisoned stream? Not that he would now, as a newborn, but what if he was older?

"What about the amorphous?"

"Zultan wants a quick death," Clary says, "and dozens of Ashes kneeling around a stream to get water is a lot faster than you trying to put poison in each of their water skins."

"Ashes?"

"Phoenix's followers."

"Ah," I say, thinking hopefully they will not rebirth her from themselves after we have burned her down. "I'll need a lot of hemlock or nightshade to create a potion with enough toxicity to kill anyone," I say, somewhat argumentatively.

"Yes, that's true," Clary replies. She studies me. "You think I'm callous, don't you?"

I avoid her gaze.

"It's okay, Anna, you can say it. I've heard it before. I've just seen too much from the incarnate—the ones who follow Phoenix, anyway—to have any pity. They'll raise their children to be just as awful."

I pause. "But aren't we better than them?"

Clary stares at me, her sky-blue eyes considering me. "We try to be. I'll tell Zultan that it's my opinion, too, that we put the poison in something only the Ashes will drink."

"Thank you."

"Before I go," Clary says, "I want to teach you a potion that you should only use as a last resort to save someone's life."

I raise my eyebrows. "What are the repercussions of using the potion?"

She puts on a pair of gloves before reaching into the herb cabinet and pulling out a black plant with silver flowers. "It must be mixed with blessed water."

"Whose blessing?"

"A soothsayer's."

"How will I know if water is blessed?"

"It will be the clearest water you've ever seen."

"Okay," I say, looking at the little black plant that seems so innocent.

"You crush the flowers," Clary says, placing the herb into a burlap sack, "and then dump it all into the water. Mix it up, then force it down the throat of the dying person. They can't already be gone, though, or it won't work. They have to have some breath or some pulse."

She hands me the sack, which I take warily.

"It's called the Storm," she explains, now peeling off her glove, "and you asked about repercussions."

I wait for her to continue, but when she doesn't, I say, "And they are?"

"As the giver of the Storm, you will be relinquishing some of your life to them."

"What do you mean?"

"If it takes five swallows of the potion to bring them back, you give them five years, but it's from your life. Life cannot just be granted from nothing."

I drop the sack onto the table, a mixture of fascination and repulsion. "I suppose there are those who you would give life to," I say quietly, "but I suspect its invention was either a mistake or the outcome of evil intentions."

"Yes," Clary replies softly, but she doesn't elaborate.

I put the sack at the bottom of my saddlebag, wondering who I'd give up part of my life for. The Rising has asked me to take life, not give it, and then I get handed a potion that will give mine to another. It seems counterproductive.

"Goodbye, Anna," Clary says, touching my shoulder. "Take care of yourself while I'm gone, okay?"

I'm left with the books and scrolls and a mission to silently kill my sister's soldiers, Phoenix's Ashes. I swear the Storm rumbles in my bag.

TWENTY-SEVEN

I hug Delilah, kiss Rowan's fat cheeks, and bid farewell to Leigha. She has decided to return to her own village to see if any of her family has survived. I turn to Redford. He leans in first, so I meet him there, wrapping my arms around his neck, entangling my fingers in the hair at the nape of his neck.

"Be safe and come back soon."

"I will," he says, the words muffled in my hair.

"I love you, Redford."

"I love you, too, Anna."

He kisses me, not like he did in the meadow, and not like at our wedding. It's more reserved, and although this slight distance hurts, I understand. It's a difficult thing to know that the one you love has loved—maybe still loves, in both our cases—someone else, even though they choose you.

Faylia stays close as they ride away, and I'm overcome with a fear that I'll never see any of them again. I can't stop the tears as my new family rides away because I'm still mourning the loss of my old family, and I'm alone again. Faylia whimpers, and I look down at her. I smile. Not alone.

❂

nna!" Zultan's voice reaches me before he does, scaring me out of my sleep and nearly my skin. It's been several days since Redford left. Faylia barks and growls, and then my door bangs open. The leader of the Rising looms in the doorway, framed by light in the hallway. "There's a pack of incarnate camped mere miles away. Past Redford's village. It's an old, burned-out cottage near a lake."

My entire body trembles from the adrenaline of being awoken, and I take a second to form my thoughts. "How old is it?"

"Why does that matter?"

"Is there a tree?"

"Are you fully awake?"

I shake my head, waving my hand at him. "I mean, is there a tree that looks like a skeleton? That looks like it's never grown a leaf in its life?"

"I wouldn't know. My scouts reported it to me. It's near a lake. Go poison the whole body of water."

"Didn't Clary—"

"Yes, she told me how risky it is, but there's only one cottage near the place, and it's burned down and abandoned. No one is coming back to it until after the war, and then we can prohibit anyone from using it. Drain it. I don't know or care. This is a huge regiment, Anna. It could cripple them."

I look at my hands. They are shaking, but it's not from adrenaline now. He wants me to poison the lake where London and I learned to swim, where we watered our animals, where we'd have family picnics on its shores.

"I don't have enough poison," I say. "That lake is deeper than it looks."

Zultan's eyebrows go down, forming a frown on his forehead. "You know where it is?"

"It's mine," I say slowly. "Or it *was.* Or it still should be."

He smiles in a nasty sort of way. "Then you and your wolf know exactly where to go, don't you?"

"I don't have enough poison, Zultan."

He throws up his arms. I've seen him in his moods before, and I've tried to be sympathetic with someone who is trying to lead a band of rebels to fight a force three times its size. Poisoning the lake—if I had enough nightshade—would be an easy victory. If the regiment is moving closer to our hideout, killing them in one fell swoop would be one less thing Zultan would have to worry about.

"I'll do the best I can," I say, trying to sound placating and not frustrated and scared.

That must be enough for Zultan because he nods and turns quickly on his heel, slamming my door behind him. Faylia and I look at each other.

"Well," I say, sighing as I drag myself out of bed, "I guess today is the day I officially make good on pledging to become a rebel."

Faylia follows me around while I pack my bag, then pads after me when I go to the cellars and into my dedicated space where I've been making poisonous potions.

"What he doesn't understand," I say to Faylia, "is I simply don't have enough of the plant to make a bigger batch."

She tilts her head, and I pat it.

"Maybe we can find more plants along the way."

When I've gathered everything that will fit into my bag, I put it on so the strap loops around my shoulder and the pouch hangs at my hip. Then, I put my cloak around me, slip on my gloves, and leave. I have no one to say goodbye to, and Zultan has already given me leave. It's close to dawn, so Faylia and I walk in the darkness close together for comfort and warmth. I'm grateful for my gloves and cloak, although I try not to think about who gave them to me.

I envision my home—my old home—and how it must look with Phoenix's Ashes camped in it. The skeleton tree will greet me as it always does, but I don't want to be welcomed. I said goodbye to the place and the family I had there.

Sun breaks over the forest, reminding me of the brilliant autumn day when Redford and I said our vows despite the decree that was about to be signed into law. My heart aches for Redford, for that day in the meadow. But I can't have that, so instead, I fight against the warsol who would rather I didn't exist or who would change me into what they are.

Faylia and I stop for a quick drink and bite to eat, then she lays on her stomach in my path and growls at me to get on.

"But you're tired, too," I protest.

She doesn't move, so I get on and, once again, I become the girl in the scarlet cloak on her wolf, slipping between light and shadow, unseen and unheard, because no one cares to look or listen for an amorphous.

We avoid the village, skirting around it because I don't want to be there again, don't want to see it. The brush is thick, so we make a small, inconspicuous camp to nap. I'd been fighting staying awake since Zultan startled me out of my sleep this morning.

When we wake, I climb on Faylia again, and we make our way closer to the village. Firelight flickers in cottages and stores, smoke spirals from chimneys, and the sounds of talking and even laughter are peppered through the streets. Faylia picks up her pace, somehow sensing my want to be away from this place. But then, all the sights of home come into view. The bend in the road, the forest opposite the inky lake, the skeleton tree outlined against the indigo sky. A lantern hangs from it, swaying slightly as if someone just placed it there. Faylia stops, and I climb from her back, pulling up my hood. She whines quietly.

"Stay here," I say, "and don't give me that look. No, I don't know what I'm doing, but I'm going to try, anyway."

She pulls on my cloak with her teeth, and I swear she growls "call," and I think I understand.

"If I'm in trouble, I will call for you. Should I whistle? I can't whistle."

She sits back on her haunches in a huff.

I try not to laugh. "I'll just yell."

She goes onto her belly and covers her eyes with her paws, and this time, I do laugh.

"I'll be fine."

She removes one paw, one beady blue eye trained on me.

I stroke her fur and kiss the top of her head, then leave with a swish of cloak. The absence of her warm body against mine sends shivers across my skin like the scattering of stars above.

A few more lanterns are lit, mostly near the stables, and a fire crackles to life in the space between the stable and the ruined cottage. I step lightly toward one of the crumbling walls and crouch, looking for water skins or ale barrels or a path the Ashes might take to the lake. Several small streams feed into the lake, mostly hidden by tall grass and cattails. I always loved the way the autumn light shone on the brown stalks, turning the green stems to yellow and the cattails to burnt orange. One afternoon, when London and I were young, Mama had stayed later than usual in the fields, and we were hungry, so I taught London that cattails were edible. We made a feast of the plant, and we both threw up later. They are an acquired taste, I think.

A shout brings me out of my memories, and I startle, looking for the source. Only a handful of crowes are in this group. It's mostly incarnate who, yet again, are making a game of turning animal and human. A coyote and a fox wrestle in the center of the clearing, nearly rolling into the fire. A woman changes to a panther, sleek and glossy and almost blending into the darkening sky if not for the sparks jumping from the fire. This startles me. Feline incarnate are something I've only heard of in stories my mother told, and I have a hard time not staring at the panther—emerald eyes, muscular body, pointed ears, and the look of a thief on her face.

Men and women laugh and shout bets and pour ale from one giant barrel. My eyes narrow as warsol take their turn to fill their mugs. I wonder how many will top off their cups, how many will abstain so they stay alert while on guard. If I slip poison in now, and the soldiers start keeling over, I wonder how long it will take for someone to suspect the ale.

This is my first time. It doesn't have to be perfect.

I wrap my cloak around me and invoke my ability to remain unseen as I move behind the stable to get to the ale barrel. The lid is loose, so I slide it over a bit so I can get the neck of the bottle that contains the poison through. My fingers tremble as I pull out the cork, and I'm grateful, yet again, for my gloves, as my shaking has caused some of the potion to drip onto the leather, singeing it, but I'm grateful it's not landing on my hands.

This will *kill* warsol.

I rock back, yanking the bottle from the barrel. My breathing comes in short, heavy gasps, and I lean my back against the barrel, trying to catch air.

These warsol would slit your throat if they saw you. They are already choking the life out of you by restricting your ability to make choices such as marriage.

The voice in my head sounds like a mixture of Zultan and Clary, with Redford's voice laid over the top like icing on a cake.

Kill them before they kill you.

I grip the bottle and dump its contents into the ale, then slide the lid back on. Emerald eyes are staring at me when I glance up, and I fall back, the bottle breaking under my palm.

TWENTY-EIGHT

he panther-woman, who has suspended herself between her two forms, slithers around the barrel. *Don't let her see me.* I squeeze my eyes shut, thinking, like a child, that if I can't see her, she can't see me. But it must work, at least somewhat, because when I open my eyes, she's looking through me, bewildered.

I jump to my feet and back up slowly. Her sharp gaze flicks around the area, where, just over her shoulder, soldiers fill their cups. I breathe out—relief, fear, a mixture of both. That breath must have let some of my guard down because Panther's eyes meet mine, and she grins, feral, feline, cunning. She stalks slowly toward me and, in the least smartest move I can make, I choose to run.

Hide.

I head to where I'd told Faylia to wait. When I reach the skeleton tree, though, I slow down, and my old play weapon, the branch London and I had christened "Femur," lies next to it. I pick it up. The lantern that hangs in the tree cracks and crashes to the ground as I slam Femur against it. Little flames erupt in the dry vegetation around the tree. Distraction is as useful as hiding. Panther screams, and I cover my ears to the shrill piercing.

"I see you, you little red wraith!" she yells.

I glance over my shoulder, seeing that the others are moving toward her, beating the flames.

But there are some who fall to the ground, clutching their stomachs, others who are vomiting onto the earth.

Faylia skids to a halt in front of me, teeth bared, eyes flashing like blue lightning. I scramble onto her back, gripping Femur, and she takes off before I can get a firm grasp on her collar, but I miraculously stay on her back. She bounds up the side of a small hill that overlooks my family's home, and that's where she stops so we can take a breath. The skeleton tree is engulfed in fire, the flames spreading to the stable, and soldiers who aren't lying on the ground in agony or near death are rushing to the lake to get buckets of water.

Panther screams again. "I will find you, wraith!"

Wraith.

Red Wraith.

Isn't that what Phoenix called me the day she revealed London to us? How ironic that the queen gave me, one of her enemies, the name that her soldier now calls me.

Faylia and I continue to the crest of the hill, then head down the opposite side, away from the flames and smoke and screams. She runs until she collapses, and we find a tree like the one we have sheltered under before, a skirt of branches hiding us. I curl into her heavily breathing body and let the tears run down my face like rain.

Hours later, after I've fallen asleep or merely become numb to my nightmares, the footsteps of an army jerk me to my senses.

"Faylia," I whisper.

She opens her eyes and sniffs, then hunches low. I cover her with my cloak as if it is the source of my magic to remain unseen.

We're tucked into a hollow between rolling hills, and I

probably wouldn't have seen the movement had I not been peering at the top of one ridge, trying to determine if we might be north or south of the lodge. This place is unfamiliar, which means we may have run too far north and west, too close to the roads that lead into the capital. My gaze fixes on the crest of the hill, where several warsol who are not dressed in the queen's uniforms move. Some crouch in the tall grass, while others scoot around on their bellies or on their hands and knees. Incarnate in animal form prowl around the amorphous, and I understand. Rising members, watching the Ashes, waiting for the right moment to attack.

After several long, agonizing moments, one of the Rising sends an arrow straight into the regiment of soldiers. Someone screams. Another voice yells orders. Faylia's body is rigid next to mine, ears flat against her head, ready for a fight.

"We can't help," I whisper. "We—I—have no weapons. As Redford so clearly stated, I'm no fighter. We should get out of here."

Faylia nods, a movement so human-like that I almost forget she is Stranded in her wolf form. We crawl out from underneath the tree. As I straighten up, a familiar gait makes me stop.

"Redford is out there."

Her eyes seek him, and she lets out a small moan. A full-on battle rages now, and I'm trembling as if I'm the one in the fight.

"I can't leave him, Fay, I can't go."

She pushes me back under the tree and wriggles in after me. In that moment, I've lost sight of him, so I spread the branches slightly and rake the field with my gaze. Clary's white-blonde hair is absent, and I wonder if she's in Adderin with Delilah, or if she went back to the lodge to Zultan. No. Zultan is here, too.

The landscape starts to make sense to me, starts to become recognizable as I scan the hollow. The lodge is south, but this road leads to the castle. It's the shorter route that some warsol from our village would take when they weren't hauling goods or traveling with small children. We never used this road because the terrain is too mountainous, and we always preferred to take the longer yet safer route on the flats. Zultan must have been counting on me killing most of this regiment, otherwise, he probably wouldn't have dared attack them in an open manner. There are still more of the Ashes than the Rising. I'm ashamed for every reason that I did and did not do the task I was given.

The captain of this regiment saunters into the fray as if she's parting the crowd at a ball. Her glossy black hair and startling eyes leave me with no doubt that she is Panther. She screams, her voice high-pitched and shrill like when in her animal form, and pulls a sword. Redford's sword meets hers.

"No!" I shout, then cover my mouth, even though I know no one will hear me over the din of the battle. Faylia grabs my wrist in her maw, not hard, but firm enough to make me wince. "He's all I have left, Fay." Her lip curls. "Besides you."

But Redford is proving a tough match for Panther. He meets her, move for move, strike for strike. I don't want to watch, but I can't tear my gaze away. She slices him on his calf, and he yells and falls, but just before she strikes, Zultan appears, parrying her killing blow.

Maybe she was drawing Zultan in by fighting Redford because the knife in her left hand cuts a smile on Zultan's throat right when Redford stands and throws her aside. Yowling, she changes midair into her feline body, the knife and sword clanging to the ground as she trades them for claws. As Redford leans over Zultan, Panther sets herself to strike.

Faylia's grip on my wrist is suddenly gone, and in a blast of black fur, she bursts from the forest, jaws snapping, fangs bared. Panther screams again, and her claws rake across Redford's back, but that is all the flesh she gets of him before Faylia's teeth sink into her throat, just like they had into Blayde's. She whips Panther's body away from Redford, who has fallen forward onto Zultan, screaming in what I imagine is agony from the deep gouges on his back.

Faylia tosses Panther nearly halfway across the battlefield, then chases after her.

Panther switches back to human, hands wrapped around her throat, and her shrill voice rises above the roar of the fight. "You are the wraith's wolf!"

Then, I lose sight of them. I trust that Faylia can fight off Panther, and I have to get to Redford. The blood on his back flows as if Panther cut canal beds into his body. I can stop his bleeding. I can save him. The Lady's mantle is in the pocket of my cloak, and it will be enough to staunch the flow until I can get him back to the lodge, where I can get him yarrow.

Hide, I think as I crawl toward Redford. I dodge flailing swords and heavy boots, still bodies that are already stiff and still-moving bodies who groan in pain. When I collapse at Redford's side, I pray to the moon that he, too, is groaning in pain because that means he will not be still and gone. My hands roam his back, checking the depth of the wounds, the width of the marks, and the number of them. Five like her claws, twice as big as their width, three times as deep as their length.

My saddlebag is heavy all of a sudden, and I feel rather than hear the rumbling of thunder.

The Storm.

I flip open the bag, hands fumbling to find the satchel at the bottom, when Redford lets out one awful choke. The Storm subsides as if it knows something, something I don't, something I dread.

"Let him survive this, let him survive this," I whisper as I use all my strength to roll him over. He has to have some breath, some pulse, I think, remembering Clary's words.

But his eyes tell me he's given up his ghost. Wide open and glassy, they stare at the sky, unblinking and bloodshot, and the light has been snuffed out.

TWENTY-NINE

I wish the screaming would stop. It's not the panther's scream. It's the wail of someone who has lost something irreplaceable. It makes my head throb and spin. The pounding paws behind me are those of a humongous wolf, not a sleek panther.

Faylia slides next to me onto her stomach. My fingers wrap around her collar, and we are thundering away from the battlefield, the dead, and the victorious incarnate. The screaming is muffled now as if cloaked by a fur coat.

It is me who screams, me whose voice clangs like funeral bells over the hollow. It becomes a choked sob, settling into my throat like a stopper in a bottle. The battlefield is a far-off memory, as though it happened in history and not to me.

Faylia collapses in the clearing in front of the lodge. I roll off her back and stare up at the sky that is dark as pitch, not a single spark of a star winking above. The lodge is quiet, curtains drawn tight against every window like lids over eyes.

"Faylia," I whisper, "you need water."

Her paws are bleeding, and she's frothing at the mouth. I help her up, and she limps along beside me. The doors are locked tight against intruders, but a trough is nearby, and I convince her to drink from it, while I cup water into my hands to clean the sore pads of her feet. Zultan couldn't have sent every last member of the Rising to the battle. We are not a big force, and I know we wouldn't all fit in the lodge at the same time, but someone has always been here.

My stomach rumbles, and I'm appalled that I'm hungry when the rest of me feels loss and ache and unimaginable emptiness. Faylia nudges me, and she must be hungry, too, so I struggle to my feet and look around for anything edible, anything that may have not yet been taken into the lodge. It gives me a purpose and excuse to ignore my pain. *Find Faylia food, save the one thing you have left.* My shin hits against something hard, and I look down, seeing that I have slammed into the cellar door. I pull on the handle, and it swings open, nearly knocking me in the face.

"Faylia," I hiss, "come."

She hobbles to me, a spasm of pain flashing over her features with every step.

"Even if the door inside is locked against us, we can stay in here tonight," I say.

She crawls inside, going down the steps mostly on her belly, and I follow, pulling the doors over the top of us. There are blankets, jugs of ale, crusty bread, and dried fruits and meats. I take several of each off the shelves and split it between us, and when I'm done, I drink without abandon, hoping I have a headache in the morning that will mask the hurt in my heart.

he low rumble of voices and the pounding of heavy boots above pulls me reluctantly from my sleep. Everything is fuzzy. The cellar ceiling, the edges of the room, the black form lying next to me. The memory of Redford's frozen eyes worms its way through the fog in my brain, and my surroundings snap into sharp focus. I'm screaming again until Faylia curls around me, and I cry until I vomit.

I've sobbed this way before. When my sister's broken body was brought home. Redford, though, won't miraculously come back to life as she did. He was not Assumed. He is truly gone.

After I've cried myself dry, I lie on my back, stroking Faylia's fur. Footsteps are on the cellar stairs, but they seem far away, so I merely turn my head in the direction of the door and stare as some of Phoenix's Ashes slide into the cellar.

"Oh!" the one in the front says. "What do we have here?"

Faylia curls her lip and growls lowly, her ears standing up along with the fur on her neck.

The other soldiers, four of them from what I can see, trip over each other and run into the lead soldier's back as they try to get into the cellar.

My movements are slow and spastic as I sit and get to my feet. I slip my hand into my cloak pocket, ensuring the bottle of poison is still there. Several jugs of ale line the shelves. I take five of them, one for each soldier, and pop off the corks. *Don't let them see the bottle.* I'm not sure if I can hide objects along with myself, but they don't seem to notice me emptying the contents of my bottle into theirs.

"Faylia," I say, "come." She pads over to me, then follows as I hand each soldier a jug. "Cheers."

The soldiers seem to be at a loss for words, and I slip around them, up the stairs, and out of the cellar. I could easily shut them in and bar the door, but there's no need. They won't leave the cellar after they drink their ale.

"Stay in the stables," I tell Faylia, "and I'll go into the kitchens to retrieve what I can." Her blue gaze fixes on me as I conceal myself before I go inside. The Ashes crawl around the lodge, inspecting every corner, looking in every room for signs of rebels. But they don't see me. The kitchen has been mostly ransacked, but a few goods remain. I fill a burlap bag, then go into the corner that was once my poison-making room. Everything is as I left it, possibly because they look like nothing more than herbs for seasonings, and what army has time to season their food when they're on the move? I dump an entire bottle of hemlock in the bottom of the water barrels, then pack everything else in another sack.

By the time Faylia and I arrive at the hollow where Redford lost his life, those soldiers will all be dead. I might not have enough hemlock and nightshade to poison streams and lakes. But water and ale barrels? I can do that.

And I do. Every regiment I find that has a supply wagon is treated to my particular form of medicine. For Redford, for the London I lost, and for Delilah and Rowan, who were forced to leave their home. For the amorphous.

THIRTY

huddle in the brush along a trail, waiting for a regiment to roll by. Not many have come through the hollow in recent weeks. The rebels are still out there fighting, evidenced by the destruction I come across when I'm stalking the incarnate soldiers. I haven't tried to contact the Rising, though. I do better on my own rather than taking orders from others. Faylia pants beside me, having run from one side of the valley to the other.

Movement in the trees to the south catches my gaze. I shift my legs, crouching lower, trying to ease some blood back into my feet. It sounds like a small group, and my heart sinks, thinking they'll be carrying their own water skins. But phoenix-badged Ashes have become scarce in the hollow, so any enemy is welcome to saunter into my domain. This place where Redford lost his life has become my haunt, my refuge. The trees where Faylia and I hid during the battle now store my herbs, and they also provide warmth and protection from the elements. While the war has been raging, Faylia and I have been silent killers, returning here for only brief respites.

Someone emerges from the trees, a blonde someone, with

hair like clouds and piercing blue eyes. No. Only one eye. The other is covered with a blue patch the same shade as her missing eye.

"Oh, my moons," I whisper. "It's Clary."

I've lost count of how many weeks it's been since I've been sneaking around the kingdom, of how many months it's been since Clary left and Redford died. Enough time that Clary has been to Adderin and returned and had a run-in with one of the Ashes. I wait until she is only five feet away from me before I emerge from the brush.

Clary draws her sword as fast as I expected, hence the reason I'm several feet away from her.

"Bleeding red planets above," Clary says. "It's the Red Wraith this entire kingdom is terrified of."

I grin, knowing that it looks unnatural because it requires effort to raise my lips. The effect, I imagine, is that it looks more like a monster trying to smile over fangs.

"They say she rides a black wolf." Clary glances at Faylia. "And wears a red cloak, and is only ever seen slithering away from camps or watching from the crests of hills."

I pet Faylia's head.

"Many of my group were scared to come here. They say this hollow is haunted, but I suspect only incarnate and crowes fall prey to the Red Wraith. Do you know how many of the Ashes have died after spotting her? She's an omen of bad luck."

"You're not keeling over."

We laugh, and Clary drops her sword to her side, then draws me in to a fierce hug. I wrap my arms around her shoulders, and tears that I thought I'd already shed well up in my eyes.

"I lost Redford."

"I know."

"And Zultan is gone."

"I know."

"It was my fault. I failed at my mission. I should have poisoned the whole company, but I was only able to poison the ale in the barrel."

"Zultan made the choice to go to battle, not you. You and I both told him we didn't think you could poison a whole regiment, but he went ahead and ordered the Rising to attack. It was too big."

While I agree with everything she said, I can't shake the guilt from my core. Redford's open eyes will still haunt my dreams, and he will never walk through the door to kiss me hello, never grin at me through his ale haze.

"Where are Delilah and Rowan?" I ask.

"Safe."

"What happened to you?"

Clary pulls away and peers at me. "What, this?" She shrugs. "I had a bit of a disagreement with a crowe. He wanted me to tell him where the Rising was headquartered and who its leader was, but I wouldn't tell him. So, I lost my eye. Also, I recently had a run-in with a panther, and she wanted me to tell her everything I know about the Red Wraith. I said I hadn't seen the Wraith. I mean, I haven't, right? I've never seen you at your work. But I thought I'd better escape before the panther decided to take my life."

I hiss at the same time Faylia growls, her fur bristling. "She's alive?"

"Last time I saw," Clary says, pushing her hair out of her face. "With both eyes, anyway."

"Faylia was certain she'd killed her."

"I don't think she's that easy to kill."

"She's who did it. Killed Redford."

Clary looks at me sharply, then with pity and shared grief. She gives me a one-armed hug. "We will avenge him."

I wipe my eyes. "Who leads the Rising now?"

Clary smiles. "You're looking at her."

"No one better."

"I don't think you'll take orders from me."

"I won't take orders from anyone *but* you," I reply.

"How do you feel about poisoning a castle feast?"

I fold my arms over my chest. "I feel pretty good about it. What are they celebrating?"

"Something to do with the princess and the prince."

My heart slams into my chest and nearly stutters to a halt. "The wedding?"

Clary glances sharply at me again, but it's a different look this time. "How long have you been roaming the kingdom?"

"I don't know," I reply.

"They're already married."

Of course they are. I've spent who knows how long in a red daze, intent on poisoning anything that wears a phoenix on their chest.

"Something else is being celebrated, and now that I've found you, I think getting into the castle unnoticed will be a lot easier."

"Can we actually win this, Clary?"

She sighs. "We can only cripple them. Maybe hold a knife to the queen's throat—or the princess's—and demand she retract the law."

We're losing. And we're doing nothing to convince the incarnate that we can be trusted because of the havoc we're wreaking, however small, on the kingdom.

"Has any other incarnate married an amorphous?"

Clary shrugs. "Possibly. It's the new law we're fighting now. You haven't heard about that, either?"

"I've been a little preoccupied."

Clary gives a half-grin, but it's not amused. "This is the brainchild of the princess. She says that the amorphous who want their rights back can submit themselves to a potion that will force them to become incarnate."

It strikes me like a pendulum, right in the chest. I growl, surprised there is enough animal in me to allow me to sound like my wolf-sister. "She went through with it."

"You knew about it?" Clary's tone isn't accusatory, but it's laced with a touch of reproach.

"I was told about it when I was held at the castle. I didn't think she'd have the knowledge to actually create it."

Clary snorts. "Well, she has everything at her fingertips. Even Skoll."

I look at her closely. Every time she mentions the castle healer, something in her tone changes. It's not quite anger, not quite sadness.

"Would she allow you an audience? The princess?"

"I don't want to see her."

"I don't blame you. But you could get in her chambers and find out if you could negotiate anything."

"What do we have to barter?" I ask, almost laughing.

Clary doesn't meet my eyes, which tells me she's holding back, something I'm missing and could only see if I wasn't focused on my one and only mission—poison soldiers.

"Well, it's just a thought. If we kill the queen and the princess, Skoll is next in line."

There's that tone again—softer, less harsh.

"And he's better?"

"I was his student," Clary reminds me. "He liked me. I think I could get him to work with us."

It seems like she's grasping for the moon with hands that are too small, arms that are too short.

"Could you do it, Anna? Kill your sister? Because we both know she wasn't raised in the castle, wasn't hidden away from everyone like Phoenix says. She's not who everyone thinks she is."

I look at Clary sharply. "Have you told everyone you grew up with her?"

"No. That's good information to use against her in the future. Although, she's not the same girl I once knew."

I pull up my hood and look straight ahead. "Agreed. My sister is already dead. If you'd like me to kill the imposter on the throne, I can do that."

THIRTY-ONE

A murder of crowes is camped by the river that flows into the lake next to the capital city. Their black tents ripple in the breeze, the phoenix flag flapping at the top of the largest one. They are the first defense into the capital. I can't understand why they serve Phoenix because she treats them almost as awfully as she does the amorphous, and they are usually the first in battle, just like they are first to defend here. Clary's one eye glows at me from the other side of the camp near the tall grasses by the river. Faylia and I hunch in the tree line closest to the camp. Our breaths come out in small puffs of fog, and I scoot closer to my wolf, needing her warmth.

But my entire body goes cold when Saffron saunters out of the largest tent and goes toward the fire, then makes an abrupt turn to the left—straight to me.

Faylia's body stiffens. I drape my cloak over us, wrapping an arm around her as we crouch lower. *Don't see us.*

"So, you have come." Saffron's frosty voice makes me shiver. I think he's talking to me, but his gaze goes above my head and into the shadows.

"You have always doubted me, Saffron."

I recognize the voice, but I can't place it. A woman's, soft but fierce.

"Can you blame me?"

The woman's sigh is so full of grief that I swear my heart breaks with her exhale. "What do you need from me, brother?"

I'm afraid of moving too much and catching their notice, but I crane my neck as much as I'm able to try to get a glimpse of this woman, Saffron's sister. She may have been with the conspirators when they burned Redford's home, or maybe she was in the group of conspirators I walked into after I stole the herbs.

What had he said that night, the night of my wedding, which now seems like a long-ago dream? "A deal for a deal. A sister." Then, after the arrow had pierced his back, "My—sister—" Each word was choked as if it was agony to speak of her. But the way he spoke to her just seconds ago wasn't filled with love. It overflowed with malice.

"I want you to get me my throne," Saffron says, "as always."

"And, as always, I tell you, the Moon Throne isn't meant to be yours."

"It is not meant to be London's, either."

"She is the queen's niece."

"That doesn't qualify her."

"What would you like me to do?"

"I want you to kill her."

"I will not kill her."

Something in the way she says this, perhaps her tone, rings bells for me, and I know who she is.

Spinning stars, Branwyn is Saffron's sister.

"You choose a warsol princess over your own brother?"

"She is a good person, and she has plans for Miadien. Plans to make it better and fair and equal."

I try not to snort when I think of London's potion to change the amorphous without their consent.

"I knew you wouldn't help me."

"There is no stronger army than the incarnate. The amorphous are nearly wiped out. Both Phoenix and London know of the crowe army you're trying to build. They will bring you down just as they will stop the amorphous. If you'd allied with the Rising, then both you and they may have stood a chance."

Saffron snorts. "I have an ally."

"Who?" Branwyn asks sharply.

"Let's just say he's royal in another land."

"You cannot mean Constellation Onyx."

"No, not him. Anyway, there are no guarantees the amorphous would have given me the throne. They're still warsol who don't keep their word, who think we're as foolish as our paison cousins, willing to serve. But, though they are on the losing side, they aren't as weak as we think. You know what I'm talking about."

"The Red Wraith."

I raise my eyebrows at Faylia.

"The Red Wraith," Saffron repeats. "Helaine is doing a *great* job at finding this scarlet ghost." His tone drips with sarcasm, thick like syrup and just as sugary.

"Helaine pounces on anything that gets in her way."

"It must be her cat-like nature." The inflection at the end of his sentence sounds as if he's amused.

But I am far from it. "Cat-like nature" can only mean the panther. My stomach drops, and my hands shake.

"Or the fact that no matter what she does, Phoenix does nothing to recognize her efforts," Saffron continues.

This doesn't track. If Helaine is one of the most ferocious soldiers in Phoenix's army, then she should be a commander of more than a regiment. Phoenix doesn't reward her for her conquests, which means Phoenix doesn't agree with them— or maybe Phoenix doesn't like Helaine. Maybe because she's feline instead of canine. I know how Phoenix feels about anything that is different from her.

"Helaine has an ill-disguised hatred of the princess," Saffron continues. "But I'm sure you know that and are observing it closely."

After a pause, Branwyn says, "I'm sure *you* could find this wraith, brother."

I'm not sure if she's trying to stroke Saffron's feathers or if she really means it.

"And take the glory from the panther? Never. Although," Saffron pauses, "I would do it for a throne."

"Saffron, you will *never* get the Moon Throne."

"Then give me the Crescent!" Saffron's voice is hot now, like a branding iron pulled straight from the fire, ready to make its mark. "The moon above knows I'd be a better judge and governor than Skoll!"

Dry grass crackles under boots, and when Branwyn speaks again, it sounds farther away. "I am innocent, Saffron, just as Skoll found me to be."

Saffron laughs, sounding almost like Eddy when he caws. "You can't fly. You're a disgrace."

The image of Branwyn's broken wing comes into my mind, and I'm disgusted that Saffron hates his sister because of something he sees as a deformity. She's plenty capable. London certainly thinks so.

"Please forgive me. I will ask London. I will ask her to grant your request." Branwyn sounds desperate and frightened, but most of all, heartbroken. A state I understand, an agony I live with every day. "When London inherits the throne, she could make you the Crescent."

"What makes you think she'll listen to you?"

It's silent for a few seconds, the only noises coming from the camp in the clearing.

"She loves me," Branwyn says, her voice soft. "Like a sister."

So, London has replaced me, too.

Then, softer. "Maybe more."

"Someone should," Saffron says, his words drowning hers and full of venom.

"Saffron, please," Branwyn says. "If I do this—*if* I can do this—will you forgive me?"

Part of me wants to stand and scream that she has nothing to be sorry for. She was born the way she was for a reason. But I stay hidden because Branwyn isn't my ally, isn't someone I need to protect, isn't someone I should die for.

"If you do this," Saffron replies, his voice low, "you'll find yourself in a cell rather than with a noose around your neck. You're only alive because you are useful to me."

"Is there nothing I can do?"

"Can you raise the dead?" Saffron hisses.

The grasses rustle in the breeze, and an animal close by scuttles across the ground.

Branwyn takes a deep breath. "I *was* the dead," she says, "but that's all I can manage. I cannot bring her back."

Saffron doesn't say anything for a moment. Then, he says, "What in the blackest planets above are you talking about? You were the dead?"

"I've tried, Saffron! I've delved into the darkest, deepest recesses of magic, and I cannot bring her back. I discovered a way to take on another's image. I've held my breath for days and days and days, but I cannot bring a dead body back to life. If I could, I would. I swear it, Saffron. I swear."

"It should have been you," Saffron snarls, "rather than her. If you can't bring her back, then figure out if you can trade your life for hers."

Even I gasp at that. Tears sting my eyes, although I'm not sure why. I didn't like—or rather, trust—Branwyn before, and tonight's conversation makes me like her even less. Her magic made me believe my sister was dead. She lay for days in the grave I helped dig while I mourned, then she crawled out of it like a ghoul. And she said my sister loves her.

But no one should ever be told it would be better if they were dead.

Saffron sweeps out of the trees, but Branwyn remains. I'm

not sure, even with the things Branwyn has done, that she's capable of cold-blooded murder, especially of a person who she and Saffron loved. It's not their mother, since she's alive and well and claiming to be princess of the crowes. Someone else close to them, then. It had to have been an accident. I glance behind me and see Branwyn prostrate on the ground, sobbing.

See me, I think, but she doesn't look up, and I don't know why I want her to, anyway.

THIRTY-TWO

A raven caws.

"Oh, you dratted bird."

Eddy, London's raven, has arrived, hovering over Branwyn like a guard, poking his beak in her business as if he was a spy messenger pigeon on duty.

"What are you going to do, hm?"

Maybe he *is* a spy, though, and he isn't London's raven, but Phoenix's. Which would mean Phoenix sends Eddy to spy on London and Branwyn because she doesn't really trust them. I don't think Phoenix trusts anyone other than herself.

I look over my shoulder. Branwyn has allowed Eddy to land on her arm, and pain flashes across her face. Eddy's grip on her arm is too tight, his talons digging into her skin. Blood trickles down her arm.

"Caw!" he squawks.

"It would be unfortunate if one of the warsol mistook you for a meal."

My mouth quirks up, and I'm afraid I'm going to laugh. Faylia looks over, interested in the suggestion.

"Anna?"

I jump, knocking into Faylia. Branwyn is looking straight at me. I'd forgotten to put my shield back up, and now I'm getting exactly what I wanted only moments ago. For Branwyn to see me.

"*Caw!*" Eddy says.

Branwyn shakes her arm, making him lose his footing and tip forward. He hangs upside down momentarily. Again, I try not to laugh, especially when he drops onto the ground in a huff of rumpled feathers.

"*Rrraaawk!*"

Branwyn and I ignore him as we stare at each other.

"Is it you?" she asks, breaking the silence.

I wonder what she's asking. Is it me, Anna, London's sister, or is it me, the Red Wraith? All the evidence is here. My crimson cloak, my black wolf.

"I best be on my way."

"Where will you go?"

I brush past her, knocking Eddy over again with the hem of my cloak. "Where I must."

When I'm several feet away, Branwyn calls, "She misses you."

I stop.

"They all do."

"Faylia," I whisper. "Let's run."

She lowers to the ground, and I climb on. We turn to face Branwyn, who once again has Eddy on her arm.

"*Sqw—*"

Branwyn effectively shuts him up by snapping his beak closed with her index finger and thumb. I can't help the smile that flashes, and Branwyn rolls her eyes at the raven. Then, Faylia takes off, rushing past them, toward the castle. Branwyn makes no effort to stop us, and we disappear into the thick of the woods.

We stop near the castle's outer walls. My cloak pockets are filled with bottles of poison, and my saddlebag is packed to the top, a heavy weight on my shoulder. I stroke Faylia's silky head.

"You know you can't come with me."

She whines softly, but she lowers herself to the ground so I can climb off.

"You know I can hide well."

She moans.

"I want you to stay well away from here."

She nuzzles my hand with her head.

I wrap my arms around her neck, burying my face in her fur. "I will find you in the hollow."

Faylia whimpers, but she licks my hand and then bounds away into the darkness. Whenever we're apart, it's like part of me is gone, and I shiver from the absence of her warmth, her very presence. I have resolved to find out why she can't change into her human form, but we have also resolved that it has to wait until after the war. My thoughts stray to Blayde, remembering how he was Suspended between his animal and human form, mostly by choice, but unable to communicate telepathically like his incarnate siblings. Which makes me think of his brother, and the knot in my stomach tightens. My orders are to kill the queen and the princess, not the prince.

The last time I came to the castle, I was stopped multiple times before being let in, even with my mother holding Phoenix's letter. Tonight, I slip unnoticed between crowe and amorphous servants, incarnate guards, and castle guests. The din that reverberates throughout the stone halls seems to be originating from the center of the castle, so I follow the noise until I reach a grand hall that is set up for a royal banquet. I've been living on what I can find in the woods, and when the scents of roasted meat and spiced fruits engulf me, I nearly forget my mission and load a plate. But then I shift my gaze to the throne at the top of the room, and seeing Greyson makes me lose my appetite. His gray tunic and midnight-blue coat make him look like a storm cloud, and a crown of moonstones sits on his silver hair, sparkling when the light from the sconces catches it as he moves.

I scan the crowd of guests instead. Clary had said to poison their drinks—barrels full of ale, pitchers of water, casks of wine. But these warsol are not soldiers, not the Ashes who fall at Phoenix's feet. There are guards, yes, but no one in this crowd is a warrior. And—my heart leaps—Mama. She's dressed in a plum gown, her black hair shining with silver under the firelight. But I don't see Papi. Of course, he's amorphous. He's probably been relegated to the stables or somewhere else as a castle servant.

London is nowhere in sight, but Queen Phoenix sits on her throne, sipping red wine from a goblet. My fingers itch to snatch it from her hand and dump an entire bottle of poison into it. I wonder who is in charge of passing the queen her drinks. That servant probably has to taste test every single cup before passing it to the queen. I bite my lip in frustration. It can't be a kill-them-all situation. Because while I've been poisoning soldiers for months on end, I've never stooped to killing innocents, regardless of what agenda they support. I won't poison anything that might pass my mother's lips.

I skirt around the edges of the room, weighing my options. Phoenix's goblet is empty now, and she impatiently motions to someone out of view. The crowd parts in time for me to see a red-haired warsol take her goblet, bow, and head to the casks. It's Papi. He fills the goblet, then winds his way back to the throne. He pulls out a spoon, dips it in the wine, and then sips it. He nods and, satisfied, Phoenix takes the proffered glass and waves him away.

My blood boils at seeing him treated this way.

A commotion at the back of the room catches the attention of most of the crowd. Several guards come in, surrounding someone. My stomach drops. They guard the dark-haired princess and escort her to her throne. All I can see is the top of her head, where a crown that matches Greyson's sits. The guards in front of her step to the side when they get to the dais, and Greyson helps her up the steps. He kisses her cheek, and she says something to him, then turns back to her adoring crowd. As she does, the cape she's wearing falls away from her body, and I understand what the celebration is for. London's stomach protrudes with the growth of a child, the next in line for the Moon Throne. I sink to the floor, dizzy and seeing stars.

I cannot—*will* not—poison an innocent child.

"Well," a voice purrs above me, "what have we here? An uninvited guest?"

I snap up my head and look directly into the cat-like eyes of Helaine, the panther. She grins at me, and her teeth glint, sharp and pointy. Then, the grin slides off her face, and a look of murder replaces it. She yanks me up by the hood of my cloak and forces me to walk through the crowd.

Disappear, disappear, disappear.

But curious faces look at me as Helaine shoves me forward. She's taking me to the throne. I try to jerk free, but her hands have claws, and they have sunk deep into the fabric of my cloak. But that is all she has hold of, so I fumble at the clasp, trying to undo it while she pushes me around the guests, who now move out of the panther's way.

Phoenix orders another drink from Papi, and Mama and London speak to each other, their heads close together. Greyson, however, notices the disturbance in the crowd and looks at Helaine. His eyes, beautiful and gray like the moon-stones in his crown, widen as he sees me. I flip down the hood, release the clasp of the cloak, and let it fall.

Stop seeing me.

Helaine shrieks her panther-scream, and the entire room stops, looking at her. Phoenix knocks the wine goblet out of Papi's hands, and Mama and London jump to their feet. Greyson's eyes scan the room, searching for me.

"What is the meaning of this?" Phoenix hisses. "Explain yourself, soldier."

Helaine growls and throws the cloak onto the ground. "There is an intruder! My queen, it's her! The Red Wraith!"

The crowd erupts in screams and shouts. Greyson runs down the steps and grabs the cloak, but I don't wait. My poisons are in the cloak, but I can't retrieve them. I run.

THIRTY-THREE

 footsteps pound behind me and thunder above me, and guards are everywhere.

Helaine's shrill scream overrides all the noise. "Get me that wraith!"

I take left turns and then rights, and then I stay straight but turn right back around.

"She went there!" someone shouts.

I must be flickering in and out of sight. My invisibility is difficult to keep in place while I'm running and trying to find my way out of this castle. I whip around a corner and slam into someone—and my invisibility shatters.

Branwyn clasps my shoulders with those big, taloned hands of hers. "Anna!"

"Let me go!"

"What's happening?"

I try to shake free of her, but her talons dig into my shoulders, and she draws blood.

"They're after you, aren't they? Who saw you?"

"Helaine did," says a voice. Greyson's. "You have to get her out of here."

Branwyn loosens her grip on my shoulders.

Greyson comes beside me, but I avoid his gaze. "I don't want to know what you're doing here with a cloak full of poisons, but I don't want to see you here again."

I whip up my head to look at him. "I don't *want* to be here," I hiss.

"Anna," he says in a tone which I assume is meant to be placating, "it's dangerous, and I can't hide you or protect you, and I won't help you."

I'm so angry that I shove my hands against his chest, making him rock back. "I didn't ask you to." My voice trembles with rage.

"If these poisons are meant for your sister—"

I yank my cloak out of his hands and push past Branwyn.

"Craaawwwwk."

"Oh, bleeding stars," Branwyn whispers, and she yanks Eddy, who has flown in from nowhere, from the air. "Shut *up.*"

"If you would have just listened to her, Anna!" Greyson says to my retreating back. "You'd know—"

I whip around. "Know *what?* That she wanted me to be the first to try her hideous potion? Has she tried it on our father?"

"Anna," Greyson says, his hands held up as if in surrender.

But I look at Branwyn, who holds Eddy's beak shut with her finger and thumb again. "I hope your brother does take the throne," I say. "I'll happily offer my services to him."

Her mouth drops open as Greyson turns around to look at her.

"That's a dangerous proposition, Anna," Branwyn says.

Before I can respond, the voice I hoped I wouldn't hear echoes down the corridor. *"Anna!"*

I close my eyes and will myself invisible.

"Come back!" London's voice is edged with pain as sharp as a crowe's talons. "Where is she? What just happened?"

"How does she do that?" Greyson asks, looking to Branwyn, whose face is pensive.

"She's used to not being seen," the crowe says softly. She looks at Eddy, who gives her a beady eye. "Sorry, darling, but you've seen too much." She stuffs him under one of her wings and says, "This will have to do until I find an unbreakable cage." Then, she looks at London. "I must go now, my princess."

I know I should move, flee this place, but the tears streaming down my sister's face keep me rooted.

"My brother is waiting," Branwyn says.

London draws in a shaky breath. "I'm afraid he cannot have it, Branwyn."

"Then, I will do what I must. Goodbye, London."

"Don't go," London says, and Greyson reaches out to steady her as she sways on her feet.

Branwyn cups my sister's face with her taloned hands. "I will always come back to you."

I see red as I wonder if London ever cried about me the way she's sobbing over this crowe-girl. Branwyn kisses London's cheek, then turns away, the feathers of her broken wing brushing the stone floor.

"Shall we travel together, Anna?" Branwyn looks straight into my eyes, but both Greyson and London stare through me. Branwyn doesn't wait for an answer and keeps walking.

I glance back at my sister. She's grasping her belly with both hands, and Greyson is holding her around her waist.

I flicker back into their vision, and London's eyes widen. *This*, I think, *is it*. I could surrender, go with London, have her pardon me. I could sit by her side, take her potion, be a model amorphous for others to follow. I could be her shadow again. Somehow, things could go back to the way they were, and I won't be alone again.

She stretches out her hand, and mine lifts toward her, it seems, on its own accord.

The panther screams from close by.

THIRTY-FOUR

ake her," London says to Branwyn. "Take her to our cave." To me, she says, "Go with Branwyn, Anna, and she will keep you safe until I can talk with you. Don't go to Saffron, Anna, please. I'm begging you."

I go to speak, but the words get dammed in my throat, and I merely let out a choke.

"It'll be okay," London says. Greyson finally releases her so she can come to me. She grasps my hand, and I flinch, not ready for her touch. She lets go quickly.

"Come," Branwyn says. "Go invisible. I'll take you to safety."

With one final look at my sister, I will myself to no longer be seen, and I follow Branwyn out of the castle. The defensive lines have doubled, and more outside lamps have been lit. They are searching for someone, *me,* but some of them shrink away from their duties, ducking into well-lit taverns.

"They are afraid of the Red Wraith," Branwyn murmurs. "They know that only death follows her presence."

"They lucked out tonight," I reply.

Branwyn chuckles, and I'm once again struck by what she finds humorous.

When the castle is far behind us, and we come close to the crowe camp, Branwyn says, "What are your true intentions, Wraith? Do you intend to stay here and wait for your sister, or do you mean to follow through with your promise to offer my brother your services?"

I stare at her. "Are you encouraging me to leave? Are you telling me you have been working against Phoenix this whole time? That you're betraying my—that you're going against the princess?"

"Phoenix is a zealot who believes that only her kind are worthy of a good life. Your sister does not believe that."

"But she—"

"Would the queen tolerate her heir thinking differently than her?"

I rub my temples, easing the pressure that has been building in my head. "No," I say quietly, "but it's still not right."

"Change can't be made overnight, Anna. You do have a choice," she says, yet again proving to me why she's so hard to trust. If she's on London's side, why would she encourage me to leave? "You could have run away from me at any time."

"I suppose," I reply, "but I have a strange notion that you can see me even when I'm cloaked in my magic."

"Wrong."

I blink.

"I can sense you."

I give one short laugh. "Okay, then you could have sensed me leaving."

"You seem a little unsure of what you want," Branwyn remarks, ignoring my comment.

"I want...." I stop because it's true. I want my sister back. Redford back. Family. But I'm not certain I want to go back to being London's sister, to standing aside while she and the incarnate turn the amorphous into something we aren't. The Rising gave me a purpose when I lost everything. It's hard to believe that a few months ago I gained a new family, a new purpose, despite my race being at war. It's even harder to believe that less than two years ago, I had a different family, one that, at the time, seemed secure. But I wasn't someone special or unique in those families, and I tried to fill in the spaces that London left empty, but I couldn't. I was, as Redford told me the night Greyson came to my house to deliver the letter from Phoenix, hiding in the grass, afraid. Behind those families, afraid.

But now everyone, including Phoenix, is afraid of *me*.

Branwyn speaks again. "Saffron's intentions were, at one time, honorable and admirable. They mirrored those of the amorphous. Treat the crowes as well as you treat the incarnate. It shouldn't be that hard, right?"

The crowes have long been associated with dark magic, most of them preferring to live their lives at night away from the sun. They, too, worship the moon like the warsol. And legend says that long ago the crowes were able to take on human form because they were given warsol blood in exchange for protection. The aeobanach and paison said it was unnatural. Their way was seen as better, since the paison took on human form by only giving a tail feather. And subsequently became enslaved to the aeobanach who bequeathed it, but that's never mentioned. The warsol and crowes said the aeobanach and paison were hypocrites. Over time, the warsol and aeobanach mended their relationship, as did the paison and crowes, since they are distant cousins. I'm not certain the crowes have ever wanted to befriend aeobanach, and they certainly dislike the yoke Phoenix has on them now.

"I know we have a checkered history," Branwyn concedes, almost as if she can see the history—or folklore—of the Laéth Realm running through my mind. "We are ruled by Phoenix but kept in check by her Crescent. Saffron believes we should be able to rule ourselves, or at least that a crowe should be the Crescent to represent our race at court."

I have to agree. It doesn't seem too much to ask. "Has London promised you that?"

Branwyn smiles blandly. "London promises a lot of things, but they are promises based on hope, not on fact."

I furrow my brow, asking myself, yet again, how true is she to my sister.

"It's politics." Branwyn gives me a faint smile.

It's silent except for the faint shouts from the soldiers and guards who comb the castle and city for the Red Wraith.

"How likely is it that Saffron would even ally with the amorphous?" I ask.

"You heard him. My guess is that he will turn you into the queen in exchange for some sort of throne or title."

"Wonderful."

"He is rather macabre."

"They've been murdering amorphous up and down the kingdom," I say, "and I'm certain the leader of the Rising isn't too keen on allying with them. They burned down my home, killed my— "

"Redford?" Branwyn asks quietly.

I shake my head. "No, that wasn't a crowe. Helaine killed him. But the crowes—your brother was the leader that night—burned down his home on the night of our wedding. The amorphous believe the crowes are puppets on Phoenix's string, but they aren't ready to forgive them for the damage they have done."

"I understand that." Branwyn looks to the camp, where crowes are flying in and out, seeking, hunting. "We are a misguided lot," she continues. "We did her bidding in the hope she'd give us our freedoms, all the while plotting about how to get out from under her thumb should she never let us go."

I study Branwyn. She is the most confusing being I have ever met. I wonder how London ever came to trust her—if she does. If Branwyn is really hers. For her part, London certainly believes that Branwyn is her ally.

Perhaps the answer lies in the conversation Branwyn and Saffron had.

"Who was Saffron talking about? The girl who was killed."

Branwyn snaps her gaze to me, her eyes glinting like fiery amber stones. She clenches her jaw, and her cheekbones pop out, sharp and angled.

I bow my head. Some things are too hurtful to reveal.

aylia must have started coming my way when she got a whiff of my scent because she meets me before I'm even close to our tree in the hollow. Her big paws knock me to the ground as she pounces on me, licking my face while also growling her displeasure.

"I know, I'm sorry," I say, laughing and pushing her away.

Faylia keeps whimpering and scratching at me. Not only has my delayed return made her upset, but Clary has appeared in the hollow's clearing. Her arms are crossed over her chest, and the way her eyebrows are slants rather than arches tells me how mad she is.

"Calm, Faylia." I stroke her head as we walk toward the leader of the Rising. "I told you I'm no good at taking orders."

Clary holds up her hand. "Not here. In the trees."

I glance at Faylia, whose upper lip curls, but she doesn't growl. We duck under the branches to find Clary with a few other Rising members waiting for us. I glance around. A lot of members are here, and they look like they're preparing for a battle.

"How did you know I didn't succeed?" I ask before any of them can talk.

"We knew you fled the castle," Clary says, "because that's what I was told."

I furrow my brow. "Who told you?"

She waves her hand impatiently. "That's the talk coming from the capital. It's all anyone discusses. The Red Wraith has been seen, and death will come shortly." Clary shrugs and nods her head toward the gathering of members in the woods. "I thought we'd take advantage of it. Others are scattered around, hiding deep in the trees. But there have been no hints that the queen or the princess has died, and with them on the throne, I don't know if I can risk the few soldiers I have."

"No," I reply. "I didn't get a chance to…." I trail off, thinking about how it's my father who tests the queen's food and drink for poison, how if I poisoned the ale barrels, Mama might drink out of that glass. How an innocent child would die if I poisoned my sister.

Like a stab in the heart, the truth punctures me. I could not actually poison my sister. I've tried for so long to fight against the fact that London abandoned her family—after she was kidnapped, I admit—to become the heir to the Moon Throne. Phoenix most likely threatened her with our deaths and Redford's and anyone else's that she loved. But I hate her changing-amorphous potion, and I don't understand her reasoning for it. But I realize I don't really know her reasoning. I'm just assuming the worst about her because she put me through the worst thing I've ever had to endure.

I sink to my knees, and Faylia, the only true companion I have left, puts her head on my bent neck. I can't let the Rising kill my sister, but I can eliminate the one who hates the amorphous.

"I will not poison the princess," I say, "but I will try to kill the queen. But it can't be by poison."

Clary lets out a huge breath. "Explain."

I lift my head. We have all lost in this war. So, I tell her about my father, my mother, and the child London carries.

"I thought when you joined the Rising that you understood your family might have to be sacrificed."

I raise my head. "My understanding has changed."

Anger flashes in Clary's blue eye. She looks to the other Rising leaders, who either stare blankly at her or angrily at me.

"Give us a moment, Anna," Clary says, her back to me.

I walk away to give her the privacy she requests, and I keep walking. Clary will do what she has to. The Rising will either succeed tonight, or they will fail, but it's not in my hands and never has been. There is no clear direction for me, save one. Killing Phoenix is the only choice I have left, leaving the throne open to someone who once loved an amorphous.

THIRTY-FIVE

t feels like I was just here," I murmur to Faylia. We watch the city at the edge of the capital's borders. Faylia gives a wolfish snort. The moon is starting to relinquish its reign, the sun slowly coloring the sky the faintest pink. The fervor of the last few days after the Red Wraith was spotted has died. Most of the occupants of both the city and castle are asleep. Except the line of crowes, although they, too, are heading to the tent after what I assume has been a long night on watch.

"Should I go now or wait until this evening?"

Faylia cocks her head, considering. She looks over her shoulder, then back to the capital, then gestures with her muzzle to the castle.

"Yes, Clary is probably livid at me for leaving, and she might be making the rash decision to try and storm the castle despite my failure to poison the royals."

I have hope that under Greyson's command, his soldiers will peacefully subdue the Rising. I wonder if London will grant me clemency for all that I have done and am about to do.

"Now or never, hm?" I say to Faylia.

I was never a fighter, and I have no weapon. My simple plan is to cloak myself in invisibility, steal a dagger, and stab the queen in her sleep.

I've made do with worse.

I rub Faylia's ears, give her a peck on the head, and then leave her in the brush we've been hiding in. An overwhelming feeling of loss engulfs me, but I chalk it up to being the normal missing-her-presence ache. I glance over my shoulder.

She crouches low, her gaze locked on me. The same fore-boding feeling I had when I parted ways with Blayde assaults me now, but I saw him again—from a distance, yes, but it was him. I'm not sure I can content myself with seeing Faylia one more time only from a distance, and I almost turn around. But I think of the child growing inside my sister, and of the Rising members who will walk foolhardily into a battle they cannot win if the queen is on the throne, so I push all my feelings aside and concentrate on not being seen as I make my way through the capital and into the sleeping castle.

The corridors are more crowded than I'd like with servants changing shifts, but by eavesdropping on their conversations, I figure out that the queen's chambers are on the top floor of the castle. A dozen guards line the corridor, but their eyes glaze over as the Red Wraith passes.

I stop in front of the door to the chambers, waiting for someone to go inside. I'll wait all day if I have to.

hide—both with my magic and behind one of the queen's grand chairs—until the sun's rays paint the sky gold. When the door finally opened this morning, Phoenix was already up. I had slipped in behind a servant, snagging a dagger from a guard closest to the door, who insist-ed the servant had taken it, who in turn protested vehemently that she hadn't, and Phoenix told them both to shut their traps, so he finally conceded that maybe he had forgotten it that day. I made myself comfortable on the floor behind the chair. For a few agonizing seconds, I thought Phoenix had seen me because her eyes lingered a bit too long in my direction.

I'm hungry and thirsty and completely exhausted, although I've dozed off several times throughout the day, only to jerk awake every time the door opened. Phoenix finally re-enters her chambers as evening falls. She tosses her cloak on her bed, then goes to the window, hands on hips, for several minutes. A light knock on the door sounds, and she sighs, making her seem almost human.

"Come in."

A servant opens the door and curtseys. "My queen, would you like me to serve your dinner here or in the princess's chambers?"

"Here."

"Yes, my queen."

She goes to shut the door, but before she can, yelling and the clanging of weapons come from the corridor. A panther leaps into the room, hissing and clawing. The servant screams and jumps out of the wild cat's path. My heart nearly claws its way out of my throat, where it had lodged the moment I heard the panther's hiss.

Helaine pins the queen to the ground, and her massive tail slams the door shut, closing it in the servant's face. Her emerald eyes glimmer in the coming darkness. Phoenix hasn't made a sound, and I marvel at her stoic indifference at being pounced on by a gigantic, fierce panther. Guards pound on the door, trying to get in, but the panther's body is strong.

"*Enough!*" Phoenix yells. "I will deal with this. Go back to your posts."

The panther grins as she changes back into a young woman.

"You do know you will be executed," Phoenix says.

Helaine shrugs. "Maybe. Maybe not."

Phoenix laughs, but it's not amused. My heart, now back in my chest, pounds so loudly I'm afraid they will hear it.

"I've been begging for a private audience with you for months," Helaine says.

"You have done nothing to earn a private audience with me," Phoenix replies.

"I had the Wraith in my claws." Helaine's tone is that of a sullen child.

"Perhaps if you had *kept* her in your claws, you would have been granted your request. But," Phoenix continues, walking over to a table while keeping her gaze trained on Helaine, "I am now curious about what is so important. Well done." She sits in a chair at her dining table, crossing one leg over the other. "You have intrigued me."

Helaine grins again. "I'm here to ask you about an amorphous named Namir. Do you know him?"

It's lucky Phoenix is sitting down because the blood drains from her face so fast that she looks about to faint. I have never heard of this warsol, but he obviously means something to both Phoenix and Helaine.

"No," Phoenix says. Even I can tell it's a bold-faced lie, and it doesn't fool Helaine, either.

"Liar," Helaine says, prowling toward the table as if she was in her panther form. "He is the only reason I'm in your service, queen. To get close to you."

"I can't imagine why."

"Can't you?" Helaine sneers.

Phoenix stares at Helaine until Helaine slams her hands on the table as she hisses like the panther she is. Phoenix appears mostly unmoved, except for her twitching fingers.

"I know that I'm not my parents' natural child. They were both amorphous, and I have been able to change into a panther for as long as I can remember. I begged them to tell me why I could change, and especially why I could change into something feline, not canine. On my fifteenth birthday, they sat me down and told me a strange story. I had been delivered to them by a man who asked that they love me and care for me.

He said he was delivering me to amorphous parents because if I turned out to be incarnate, they wouldn't love me less, but if he delivered an amorphous to incarnate, I would be shunned."

Phoenix's chest rises and falls rapidly, but still, she doesn't speak. I shift my feet, and both Helaine and Phoenix look in my direction.

Hide, hide, hide.

Helaine must decide it's a trick of the light because she continues. "My father followed that warsol into the dark of the forest and saw him speak with a prince. Falcon."

"My brother's dealings were his own," Phoenix says.

Helaine continues as if Phoenix hadn't spoken at all. "Falcon called him by the name of Namir and told him that it was time for him to either die or return to the Norgate."

Phoenix's trembling hands curl into fists.

"What is the Norgate, Phoenix?"

"Why would I know that?"

Helaine gives one small laugh. "Humor me with a guess. You, a queen of the Laéth Realm, would know all its deepest, darkest secrets, wouldn't you?"

Phoenix returns the smile and, by all appearances, it would seem they are having a pleasant conversation. "It's a passage between realms," she says, placing her fisted hands into her lap.

Helaine sits back hard in her chair. "Other worlds?" she whispers.

"Some believe so. Old religion practitioners."

"Do you? Are you one of them?"

"No."

"Did Namir go?"

"How would I know?"

Helaine's eyes glitter like green fire. "Because you are the only one who would know, now that Falcon is dead and there are no traces of Namir, except the one that leads to you."

I look to the queen. Phoenix breathes heavily through her nose and blinks rapidly.

"Feline warsol are rare, aren't they? The only conclusion that I can come up with is that whoever Namir was, he was a feline warsol and my real father. But why would Falcon want to get rid of him? And then I got to thinking." Helaine taps her chin. "What do Falcon and Phoenix hate the most?"

Phoenix jumps to her feet, but Helaine is quick. She leaps onto the queen again, her movements sleek and swift. She pulls Phoenix down and crawls on top of her, her hands now adorned with the claws that belong to her panther body. She resumes the conversation as if she's not holding down the queen by force.

"Amorphous. So, Namir had to have been an amorphous but had panther in his bloodline. But why would Falcon care? He would only care if my existence was somehow a blight on his royal family. Who am I, Phoenix?"

Phoenix stares at Helaine. "You are my daughter, Helaine."

I slap both of my hands over my mouth, willing myself not to shout.

Helaine shrieks and morphs completely into panther form, slamming into Phoenix. But Phoenix is a wolf, and her canine body bursts out. Helaine swipes at Phoenix with her clawed paw, but Phoenix dodges and clamps her jaws around Helaine's throat, then tosses her across the room. Helaine's wounds look like giant craters in the moon, deep and wide. She fades almost entirely back into her human form, but she is Suspended, her legs and arms that of a panther but her face a human's.

Phoenix stalks toward Helaine, almost cautiously. She tilts her head, inspecting her victim.

"I tried to serve you well, Mother." Helaine presses her hands against her throat, but it's too late. Her body goes rigid, and Phoenix stares at the daughter she refused to raise, refused to even acknowledge. As if in slow motion, Phoenix shimmers back into a human.

"Help," she whispers, kneeling next to Helaine. She looks around wildly while putting pressure onto Helaine's wounds.

I let my facade drop, and I crawl around the chairs.

"Queen?"

Phoenix turns, her face full of horror and grief. "My daughter," she says, gesturing to the dying girl on the floor.

I rush to Helaine's side. This is the girl who killed Redford.

"Please," Phoenix says, her hands trembling.

I brush away Helaine's dark hair and inspect her wounds. It's too late. Helaine gives one last shuddering breath and then is still.

I close her eyelids and look at Phoenix. I don't have to tell her what she already knows. She stands, backing away. And then the Queen of Miadien slams her right hand onto the left side of her chest, collapses, and stops breathing.

THIRTY-SIX

y first thought is a horrid one. *My job is done, and I didn't even have to raise a dagger.* After several long, silent moments, a tentative knock sounds on the door.

"My queen?" a male voice asks. He knocks again. "Is everything all right in there?"

Muffled voices, one higher in pitch, argue quietly, and then the door opens. The paison servant who earlier had been accused of stealing the dagger enters the room and gasps.

I burrow into my invisibility and go behind the chairs again.

"What?" the male guard asks, shoving his way in. He stares at the corpses on the floor. "Get the princess." The paison makes no movement to obey, and the guard puts his hand on her shoulder. He pushes her softly out of the room and comes over to the queen. Bruises and scratches are peppered over her body, but nothing looks like a mortal wound. Except for the fact that she's dead.

Several more guards move in, and then I hear the paison's voice and another I recognize. Mama enters the chamber. She shoos everyone away from the two dead women on the floor. I'm surprised at her reaction. She claps her own right hand to the left side of her chest but, thankfully, she doesn't stop breathing. She sinks to her knees and places her left hand over Phoenix's heart and closes her eyes.

Anger flashes through me at the sight of my mother mourning the queen. She killed the queen's brother, the father of her first child. Mama, it seems, is as bad as incarnate come, right up there with Phoenix herself.

"Retrieve the princess," Mama says.

The guard I'd stolen the dagger from says, "She's on her way."

"Say nothing about this to anyone. This stays here, do you understand?" Mama's gaze is fierce on the servants and guards, and they nod.

"Yes, Queen Mother," says one guard softly, and Mama snaps her head in his direction.

That's right. London is now the queen.

Mama cleans off the blood from Helaine's throat and, even in the haze of anger, I realize how much I've missed her, and that maybe, just maybe, she had to kill Falcon to keep London safe. I just want to be close to her again, to smell her scent of rosewater, to see her don her fox fur.

The chair slides a little as I stand, making a small scratching noise, but no one pays it any mind because their focus is on Phoenix and Helaine. I slip between two guards to get a better view of my mother. Her face has lines that weren't there before, and her mouth trembles slightly as she cleans and situates the bodies.

"Mama," I whisper.

She stops, glances up, and I want her to look at me so badly that I drop my curtain, and she finds me. Just for a second, and then I gather my cloaks—magical and scarlet—around me.

"Anna?" Mama says, then blinks rapidly.

London enters the room, and Mama's focus turns to her. My sister's face is drawn and pale, and she looks a bit puffy. She squints in the firelight as if she's having trouble seeing.

"Phoenix?" London whispers, but I don't want to know

if she, too, mourns the queen. I crawl on all fours, dodging guards' boots and servants' shoes, and scuttle out to the corridor. As I get to my knees, the sight of gray boots and dark blue breeches makes me stop, and I find Greyson, his tunic wide open and his hair disheveled.

He stops and looks down, tilting his head slightly.

I pull up the hood and turn my face away.

Just like I did to Clary, I stand and walk away and don't stop or look back. When I get to our hiding place, Faylia jumps up, and I climb onto her back.

"She's dead," I say, and Faylia takes off into the dark of the woods. We go back to our hollow—rather, what was once our hollow now that the Rising has taken up residence in it. Some of the soldiers go to drag me off Faylia and arrest me, but Clary comes into the clearing and stops them.

"The queen and the panther are dead," I tell her. "But my sister and her husband are strong, and you will not stand a chance."

Clary gives a half-smile, then she commands her Rising rebels to get into formation. But Faylia and I keep going. Clary thinks I killed the queen, but the queen was killed by her own hand. By her own broken heart. If I had done it, I wouldn't have done it for the Rising.

We leave the sanctuary of our hollow. It seems all I can do is keep going because if I stop, I'll lose what will I have left to live.

he guard at the Istreyan border scowls at the ragged band of amorphous civilians as they approach. Faylia and I wait near them, cloaked in my invisibility.

"No Miadiniens," he says before anyone can speak, holding up his hand.

"But you have to let us in," says the older woman who stands trembling with a heavy pack on her back.

"By order of His Majesty, the Constellation Onyx, no foreign races allowed in our lands due to the need to keep His Royal Highness, Star Silverstone, safe."

A young boy, probably in his early teens, snaps, "So, you'll let hundreds die due to war in our kingdom to protect one child?"

The guard stiffens. "He is not just a child. He is our Star."

From what I've gathered from snippets of conversations I've heard over the years, and more recently during my travels, Onyx and Sorrene, his wife, were childless until a year ago. Rumors of infertility, other rumors that Onyx was in love with a paison, even more that Sorrene's brother, Pala, forced her to marry Onyx so he could become a royal. But Sorrene finally conceived and gave birth to the new prince. She died shortly after.

"Why were you taking refuges before?" the teen asks.

"Your kingdom was experiencing skirmishes but now is in a full war."

"We have been for months, and we are not a danger to your Star. Why would we be?"

The guard eyes him. "Orders are orders. Now leave."

The amorphous refugees turn away, but not before the teen gives the guard a look and rude hand gesture. With the guard's attention focused on the petulant teen, Faylia and I walk right past him and through the border gate. It slams shut behind me, trapping the guard in Miadien land. He yells something unintelligible to the band of amorphous, then he shouts at his fellow guards to open the gate and quit messing around.

It makes me smile for the first time in who knows how long, but with each step that takes me deeper into Istreya and farther from Miadien, the knowledge that I've left my country, the only home I've ever known, trickles over me like icy rain. Something in me says I will not see it again for a long time.

But Delilah and Rowan are somewhere in Adderin, and the fastest way there is through this border gate. I intend to find them. But the more I wander, the more lost I become. We make camp in a cave near the Adderin and Istreyan border, near the shimmering Silver Lake. But I must have taken the wrong road because I find myself closer to the Edges, so I go west again and make a home in the ancient paison caves.

For days, weeks, months, I watch. And I listen.

I drop my invisibility, certain no one is looking for me now. But then, I hear something.

"Anna."

My shoulders stiffen. With my back to the mouth of the cave, I can't see who has just spoken my name, but I would know the voice anywhere.

THIRTY-SEVEN

reyson stands just outside, wrapped in a dark gray cloak. A lump on his chest under the cloak squirms and makes a small, whimpering sound. I gasp, bringing my hands to my mouth. Greyson smiles and pulls the cloak down, and a round face with a head of fuzzy red hair pokes out.

"We named her AnnaGrey," he whispers.

I snap my gaze to his but bring it immediately back to the baby. My niece. With one finger, I stroke her little pink cheek.

"Why are you here?"

"The castle is under siege."

"The Rising?" I ask, incredulous.

"No," Greyson says. "The crowes."

AnnaGrey gives one short, little cry. Faylia pads over to me, curious.

"Do you want to hold her?" Greyson doesn't wait for my answer. He unwraps his cloak, revealing a harness he carried AnnaGrey in. Something silver slips out of the cloak's pocket and clatters to the ground. I pick it up, noticing it's the same symbol he wore when I first met him—except it's not. This one isn't a phoenix. It's a wolf, mid-howl. The sign of the new queen.

He pulls the harness from his shoulders, gently cradling AnnaGrey's tiny body as he does. Then, he passes her to me, and I take her in my arms, and the rush of feelings that engulfs me takes me by so much surprise that I gasp. AnnaGrey yawns, breathes, nuzzles in her blankets, and my heart is in danger of being stolen.

"Oh, moonbeams, Greyson."

"Can you keep her safe for us?"

I look at him quickly. "You want me to keep your child?"

"We should sit," Greyson says, leading me by the elbow to the fire pit I'd built for the cave.

I settle against the cave wall, and Faylia snuggles next to me. Greyson sits across from us and starts a fire while he talks.

"The Rising was subdued some months back. They tried to lay siege to the castle, but the incarnate were just too many and too strong, even with Phoenix dead along with Helaine." He stares at me as if he wants me to admit something, but I have nothing to tell. I keep my gaze focused on the tiny being in my arms. He sighs softly but continues, telling me how some amorphous escaped, some were killed or wounded, and others were taken prisoner.

"The leader—"

"Clary?" I interrupt.

"The one-eyed blonde. Yes. She surrendered to save what was left of her amorphous army. In the confusion and disarray of their surrender, Saffron and his crowes turned on us, incarnate and amorphous alike. Vermilliana was killed, and Saffron named himself prince of the crowes.

"London was in no condition to lead another battle. The stress was too much for her, and Skoll recommended the baby come early. Amethyst gave her a potion to start labor. She nearly died, while Skoll and I tried to fight back the crowes."

I glance up. "Where was Branwyn in all this?"

"With your sister, where she remains. No one except Branwyn knows that this child was born alive."

I hold AnnaGrey closer to my chest, breathing in her newborn scent. "Did London ask you to bring her to me?"

"Yes."

"Even after…."

"Yes."

"What about my mother and father? Why can't they keep AnnaGrey safe?"

"They can't hide like you can." Greyson rubs his hand over his face, his fingers lingering on the beard he now sports.

Faylia hasn't moved, and he looks down at her.

"She's Suspended."

"Stranded," I correct. "Your brother looks Suspended."

"Blayde," Greyson breathes. "When did you last see him?"

"The night of my—the night I—" I stop, finding it difficult to talk to Greyson, of all people, about my marriage. "The night my wedding was ambushed by Saffron. Blayde and Faylia were together for a time, but because she is Stranded, I can't determine what happened to him. I hoped to find him, but I've seen no sign of him in my travels. I've waited too long to come to find Delilah and Rowan. My mother- and brother-in law," I say, seeing the confusion on Greyson's face. "I never met your mother. I'm sorry, I don't know her fate."

"Blayde has been Suspended for a long time," Greyson says. "He can turn wolf, and he used to be able to turn fully human, but lately, he remains in a combination of skins. I last saw him when he delivered my mother to the castle for the wedding."

"He saved me," I say, not looking at him, but at my niece. "I wanted to find him, too. He didn't stay for the wedding?"

"We thought it might be a bit too dangerous for him given that his loyalties were never certain. He left, even though I didn't want him to. I would have protected him."

"He would have felt caged."

Greyson nods. "It seems you got to know him well."

"No," I reply. "It's just that he showed his heart and his spirit even through the fur."

"Maybe he left Miadien, too," he says, his voice soft.

AnnaGrey gives a little whimper, and Greyson pulls a bottle from his pack. "Cow's milk. I will help you find another mother cow before I leave."

I give AnnaGrey the bottle, rocking her. I stroke her soft, red hair, marveling at how its shade is close to mine, even though mine comes from Papi, and hers must come from Greyson's side.

"What happened to the members of the Rising?"

"London has promised that all the amorphous will go free if they fight against the crowes. Clary had yet to give her answer before I left."

"We didn't part on the greatest of terms," I admit, "but I believe her heart is true, even if her mind is misguided. She's a brilliant herbalist."

"Skoll has vouched for her," Greyson says.

Not for the first time, I wonder if there is something more between Clary and Skoll, what Skoll's ultimate agenda is. But he's helping London and Greyson now, so I don't dwell on those thoughts.

"But," Greyson continues, "she also said that because of Anna, London has her loyalty."

A warm sensation, like slipping into a bath, flows over me, and I smile.

"London has sworn that the crowes will be banished forever to the Edges. Branwyn convinced London not to execute him or any of the crowes."

"Banishment doesn't mean he won't return," I snarl. "Why did she do that for Branwyn?" Jealousy flares inside me. "Why does London love her so much?"

Greyson looks at me for a long minute. "I think, Anna, that London loves Branwyn in the same way I…." He pauses and clears his throat, and my heart jumps inside my chest. "Look… we know it's a risk. It's why we need you to keep our child safe."

"You want me to raise her in this cave? I can't keep her safe."

"Please, Anna. I know what you can do. You can hide, and you can hide Grey."

I flick up my gaze. "Branwyn told you."

"No. I figured it out."

"How?"

He smiles, just a small curve of his lips. "I'm the one who told you that you could do it."

I remember the last conversation we had before the war started, before I was a rebel and he was a prince, when there was a fractured piece of hope that we could have been something. Something more than this.

"And because of the times you let your guard down." Greyson eyes me. "I know you're the Red Wraith, whose reign of terror magically ended these past few months. Rumor is that you were killed by the panther, and because she didn't bring you in alive, Phoenix had her killed."

"Do London and my parents know?"

"London does. Your mother suspects it. I don't think your father knows."

"It's probably best that he doesn't. And anyway, the Red Wraith is dead." I look down at AnnaGrey again. She's so incredible—her tiny nose, her little mouth. "I'm just Anna now. And I have a new purpose. Keeping your child safe."

THIRTY-EIGHT

The four of us make an interesting traveling party. A prince, a rebel, a Stranded Edge-wolf, and a newborn princess, the Moonbeam to the throne. We're in search of a cow or even a goat, anything that will provide milk for AnnaGrey. Greyson had at first insisted that he go alone, leaving AnnaGrey, Faylia, and me in the cave. But I'm the one who has lived here for the past few months, and the roads and paths are familiar to me.

"I'm going to have to steal it," Greyson says, and I grin at him. "What?"

"I'm not the only one who does illegal things."

He snorts.

We haven't touched on the subject of us yet. The first night, as he took AnnaGrey and swaddled her, he did whisper that he was sorry about Redford. I had merely nodded and looked away.

"Phoenix made us—" he had then started, but I'd held up my hand.

"I've heard, but I don't want to hear anymore. Let's focus on saving AnnaGrey."

"Yes. You're right."

It's not like there was anything promised or even said before.

It's late afternoon now, and we find ourselves at the entrance of a thick, dark forest, one that even I am unfamiliar with.

"I don't think there will be a cow in there," I murmur.

A rumbling sound comes from my left, away from the forest. Dust clouds billow on the road around a battalion of Istreyan soldiers. The leader is a pale aeobanach, and even though he's not tall or big, he's commanding.

"Spread out!" he shouts, and the Istreyan soldiers scatter, apparently searching for something.

"It would be wise for us not to be seen," Greyson says, "even by the aeobanach."

We duck into the thickest part of the trees, and I'm reminded of all the times I spent in the underbrush as a rebel, hiding, watching, waiting.

The soldiers comb the area, zigzagging across the land, in between the trees, under the brush, and even high up in the branches. A group of soldiers heads directly for our hiding place, and we scurry out as quietly as possible. Greyson has given me AnnaGrey to hide with my magic, and Faylia has learned to stay close by my side. If the soldiers are looking hard enough, they may see Greyson, but they won't see the rest of us.

"Find anything?" The voice is cold like frost, sharp like an icicle. I glance over my shoulder. The pale aeobanach leader doesn't have to shout to capture the soldiers' attentions.

"No, sir," one says, taking a moment to mop his brow.

The leader gives what I can only call a smirk, but I don't understand it. I suppose this is some sort of training game he's devised, and he's pleased that he's tricked his own soldiers.

"The Star is lost," he says.

I glance at Greyson quickly. He shakes his head, looking as confused as I am.

"Sir?" another soldier asks.

The pale leader bows his head, studying his hands that are clasped together as if in prayer. "I do not believe he will be found."

"Has their prince gone missing?" I hiss.

Greyson shrugs.

"Move out," the pale leader shouts, and the soldiers march away from us. I breathe a sigh of relief that we are fine, but I'm perplexed. Miadiniens were refused entry into Istreya for reasons regarding the Star's safety, and now it appears the child is gone. I shiver, thinking of the pale leader's voice.

"Where did you all come from?"

Greyson and I whip around. I had dropped my guard, and the four of us are visible to an aeobanach who stands feet away from us. She's tall, with dark red hair that looks like it has streaks of various colors in it, wide teal eyes, and white skin. She almost looks like she's glowing.

"You're not, by chance, trying to kidnap a baby, are you?" the aeobanach says, looking pointedly at the bundle I carry on my chest.

"She's my baby," I say quickly, "not the lost Star."

The aeobanach nods. "I didn't think so. Why would warsol want an aeobanach prince?"

"We're just hunting," Greyson says, holding up his hands. "I'm—Linden."

I look at him, but don't correct him. My heart hurts, though.

"And this is my wife...."

"Delilah," I say quickly.

The aeobanach cocks her head in thought. "Is that a common warsol name?"

A trickle of cold runs down my spine. "I suppose so. Have you met another warsol named Delilah?"

"Yes."

My heart leaps. "Where is she? I know her, I—"

"She took refuge with a group called the Galaxia. I'm sorry, however, to report that she became ill and has passed away."

Tears sting my eyes. "And her child?"

"The coyote pup is safe with my people."

I furrow my brow. "He's already changed?"

The aeobanach nods. "He misses his mother. The pain of loss is easier to handle in animal form."

I breathe out my grief, my chest aching. Baby Rowan is all alone except for this aeobanach and her Galaxian group.

"Who are the Galaxia?" Greyson asks. "Are they responsible for the Star's mysterious disappearance?"

"No," the aeobanach says softly. "We're a group of aeobanach and paison who don't quite agree with the way the throne has been passed down by bloodlines. If you'd like to see Delilah's pup, I can take you to him, offer you a place of safety with the Galaxia, if you're in need of it. But you must first meet with our leader and gain his approval."

Greyson glances at me. We both know it would be better if no one knows who we really are. The fewer who know about us, the better.

"How far away is your home?" Greyson asks.

"In the mountains in Adderin. It will take some to get there."

"Why aren't you there now?" I ask, suspicious.

She smiles. "I'm looking for warsol who are looking for Coyote." She walks away, glancing over her shoulder. "That's what we call Rowan. Many of us have never met a coyote warsol, as the dominant form seems to be wolf."

Greyson and I glance at each other.

"I have wanted to find Rowan," I say softly. Maybe he'd be a good playmate for AnnaGrey. That is, if I keep her long enough to see her grow out of infancy.

The aeobanach nods. "Then come. We can camp tonight in this forest. Pala and his goons won't be back."

"Was that the pale leader of the soldiers?"

She nods. "I'm Rain, by the way."

The name is familiar, but I can't place it. Greyson follows as she heads deeper into the forest, so I do, too, making sure

Faylia is by my side. Our quest for a cow or goat is now gone, but maybe the Galaxia has resources. After several moments, I remember where I've heard the aeobanach's name before. "You know Clary."

Rain looks back at me. "Yes. The Galaxia has given aid and support to some Miadiniens."

"So, you met Redford, Rowan's older brother?"

"Briefly," Rain replies. "I've been wondering if he'll come for his brother."

Greyson's eyes are on me, but I don't meet his stare. AnnaGrey's breathing is a salve to my aching heart.

I say quietly, "He's dead."

"I'm sorry," Rain says after a pause, and I can hear in her voice that she truly is.

We travel for nearly an hour before we come upon a place suitable to camp. AnnaGrey is fussy, but I'm at a complete loss as to what to do.

I rock her, put my pinky in her mouth, and am in near tears when Rain asks, "Is she hungry?"

I nod.

"Are you not able to feed her?" Rain asks.

I look up at her, stricken. "No."

Rain holds out her hands, but I hold AnnaGrey close to my chest.

"It's okay," Rain says softly. "I'm a mother, too. My youngest is a filly named Iris. I still have milk. May I feed her?"

I nearly burst into tears in gratitude. Rain cuddles AnnaGrey close, murmuring soft words to her. Faylia nudges me with her nose, and although Greyson offers me his hand to help me sit next to the firepit, I refuse and sink down next to Rain. Faylia settles at my feet, and Greyson, looking wounded, though I cannot fathom why, rekindles the fire.

Rain hands me AnnaGrey, and I pat her back and rock her. My eyes meet Greyson's from across the fire. I struggle to my feet, then go to him and place his daughter in his arms.

"My Moonbeam," he whispers.

I return to Faylia's side, and Rain, says, "You're not married, are you?"

"What makes you say that?"

Rain looks at Greyson, who hasn't heard what she said, and replies, "Because you look at the child, and he looks at the child, but you don't look at her together as someone you both created."

I go to speak, but Rain waves it away.

"It's not my business, not-Delilah. I'm going to rest."

She lies down and curls up in a blanket. She's soon asleep, and I ease into Faylia.

Greyson coos at AnnaGrey, and when he sees me gazing at them, he manages a small grin. "Go to sleep. I'll keep watch."

THIRTY-NINE

'm ripped from slumber by the shrieking of a crowe. Sleep clings to my consciousness as I reach for Faylia and try to make us invisible.

"You cannot hide from me, Anna," says a voice I know, one I have dreaded hearing again. Saffron, the prince of the crowes, is in our campsite.

Faylia growls, and Rain squats near the fire, holding a sword in each hand. I shake my head to clear my mind, then rake my gaze across the clearing, seeking my niece and Greyson. He holds her in both of his arms, and a crowe flanks him on each side.

"What do we have here? Prince Greyson, holding a new-born child? The queen is telling everyone that the child died. I already knew that it lived. She's lying to protect the Moon-beam, but that child will never be safe from me." Saffron laughs, then turns to me. "Of course they have run straight to you for help. They betrayed your entire kind, but when they need something, who is the first person they go to? The one they think is useless."

Tears prick my eyes because he's right.

"But I could have placed bets that you would abandon the

Rising for them," Saffron says, sneering. "You were only too easy to track, Red Wraith, even with your invisibility trick. Your soft, sweet heart that spared my life also gave up the life you built for yourself in exchange for your treacherous sister's child, and I followed it like a scent."

"Stop."

He cocks his head. "Truth hurts?"

I grind my teeth. Truth doesn't matter anymore. But it does hurt. The way he talks about sisters makes his hurt apparently clear. The girl he and Branwyn both loved must have been their sister. "A sister for a sister," he had said when he was dying. When I saved him.

"You would know," I snarl. "Your sister, the one you actually loved, died, and you have spent your life seeking retribution. What I don't understand is why you make the warsol pay."

"The warsol who govern us let Branwyn go! Skoll, that weak Crescent, didn't believe it was murder!" Veins bulge in Saffron's forehead and neck. His breathing is heavy, his entire body trembling. He runs his long fingers through his dark hair, and something inside me aches for him, makes me reach toward him. It must startle him because he jumps back, staring at me.

"I know you're hurt," I say. "But there are other ways to fix the pain."

"How little you know. You never even *realized* that Skoll was the true leader of the Rising, that he has been working against Phoenix to get her off the throne. That blonde coyote was his puppet."

Something cold trickles into my stomach. "How can that be? He helped save London from dying."

"I said he worked against Phoenix," Saffron snaps, "not your sister. But she was loyal to Phoenix, wasn't she? Same as my traitorous sister."

"She told you where I was, didn't she?" I ask. "Branwyn."

Saffron chuckles darkly. "No. But I am drawn to you because you had my life in your hands, and you didn't take it."

I growl. "I should have."

"Oh, Anna. You really don't know much, do you?" He glides over to me and cups my face with his cold hand. "You and I are so similar. Let's take down our sisters together. Let's vanquish the Rising and get Skoll out of the Edges. I will make you the princess of the warsol, and we will never be pushed to the sides again. You can keep the child as your own if you want. I have children, too. Twins. Perhaps they could be play-mates. It doesn't matter to me as long as she is out of my way."

I stare up into his red eyes, imagining myself on a throne next to him. I never wanted that, but I did always want a place where I was seen.

His hand remains on my cheek. It's warmer now because of the heat on my skin. "I knew we were made of the same things, Anna, the moment we met. I have not forgotten that you saved me and the promise I made. I will keep that promise and more."

"I—" Something deep, dark, and magical inexplicably draws me to Saffron. I am a moth to his flame, drinking in the elixir that his is aura. Revenge must be the sweetest wine when drunk with him.

He takes my left hand, his talons running over the ring Redford placed on our wedding day. He slips it off.

"Wait—" I try to argue, but the words are broken and choked when he puts the ring on his smallest finger on his left hand. Then, he leans in, and—

A spark of silver flashes in the corner of my eye.

"Greyson," I say, and Saffron's eyes turn to flames. He toss-es me away from him, and I land in a heap on the ground.

"You choose them," he hisses, his words hitting me like spittle. To Greyson, he says, "Give me that baby."

"No!" I scramble to my feet and run toward them.

Saffron holds out his wings, blocking me from Greyson and AnnaGrey. He gives Greyson a mocking bow. "Ok. We'll do it another way. Hand the child to your… sister-in-law." He throws a grin at me from over his shoulder, and I know because of how I whispered Greyson's name only seconds ago that I had laid bare my heart, that it told Saffron exactly how to conquer me. But that doesn't matter now.

All that matters is AnnaGrey.

Greyson unwraps the harness from his body, then hands her to me. I hold her close. Faylia winds around my legs, eyeing Saffron. Rain remains in her crouched position.

Saffron slides a long knife from the depth of his feathers and positions it under Greyson's throat. I suck in a breath, and Saffron looks at me. "Are you sure, Anna?"

But he doesn't wait for me. He draws the knife across Greyson's skin, and I open my mouth in horror at the same time Rain screams. Everyone, including Saffron, jumps at the sound. Faylia yelps, and I hold AnnaGrey closer, my heart beating madly in my chest. Rain has taken out two crowes with one swift movement of her two swords.

I expect to see Greyson on the ground, life bleeding out of him, but he is on his feet, and he headbutts Saffron and takes his knife, stabbing one of the crowes who guards him in the side.

"Run, Anna!" Greyson yells.

Faylia and I take off, winding our way through trees and brush. Wings beat behind me, and I'm picked up by black talons. I scream. Faylia stands on her hind legs, stretching to her great height, and locks her jaw around my ankle, drawing blood, and yanks me out of the crowe's grip. His talon scrapes one long deep channel along my arm, and blood spurts like a geyser.

Saffron lands on the ground, his wings splayed, breathing heavily. "Sisters are the worst, Anna," he pants. "They are nothing but wasted space in a nest."

"No." I clutch AnnaGrey to my chest, drawing Faylia next to me. "They are blood and bone and even magic in the fabric of what makes us who we are. Branwyn loves you, Saffron, and she will do anything to earn your love back. But she shouldn't have to. *That's* what makes us different, Saffron."

He can never hurt anyone I love. That is how Greyson survived. Because I love him. Saffron can never hurt AnnaGrey because I love her already. We don't need to run or hide from Saffron. As long as I am living, he can't hurt them.

"You will never touch London because while I may hate her at times, may not understand her intentions or plans, I still love her. You see that as a weakness. But it is a strength."

One that could have brought the amorphous and incarnate together possibly. All my mistakes try to flood over me, but AnnaGrey is a dam to them all. She is my redeemer, and I will protect her in the way I couldn't protect my kind. I will protect her because she is my blood. My family. A gift given to me when I had lost everything.

Besides our staggered breathing, the only noises in the wood are the scuttling of insects on the ground, the soft hooting of owls above. The clangs and shouts of the fight are distant.

Saffron glances at my bleeding arm. He inspects his talon, which has a streak of blood on it, and the red against the black makes it look almost purple. He uses my ring to clean off his talon, and the gold band now looks like it has ruby gems in it. He holds up his hand. "I will always know where you are, Anna of the Foxes—"

He is cut off by a branch that clubs him on the back of the head. His eyes lose focus, and he stumbles, reaching for me as if asking me to help him. Or catch him. His body slams into mine, our legs tangling, my arms still around AnnaGrey.

I twist to avoid falling on her, and my hair catches in Saffron's feathers as we crash to the ground. I scoot away from the crowe, whose eyes are closed, but he's still breathing.

Greyson, chest heaving, reaches to help me up. He must have lost his weapons, but the branch did the job. He's followed closely by Rain. She dashes ahead, so we follow. AnnaGrey hasn't made a noise, but she's breathing, and I cradle her head and neck against me. Rain glances over her shoulder to ensure we're following her, and she runs directly into a tree and falls.

"Rain!" Greyson shouts.

The tree she ran into begins to light up with a silvery luminescence. The tree across from it, its path-partner, shimmers into gold.

"What in the blackhole?" Greyson mutters.

Wings flap above us, and I crane my neck. *Please don't let it be the crowes.* But it's not. It's a red paison, and she's studying us curiously. She, too, is carrying something—or someone—in a bundle on her chest.

"Who are you?" I shout, but then more wings beat above us.

Saffron, blood dripping from his hair, and one of his crowes enter the clearing.

Faylia leaps at the other crowe, who is closest to us, and Saffron throws himself at Rain. She transforms into her equine form, using her antlers like swords as she swings them toward the crowe. The light in the clearing is almost brighter than the sun at noon now, and it blinds me. Greyson finds my hand.

"You have to hide, we have to go, you have to hide, we have to—"

A crowe caws, and by the light of these trees, I see Rain lying motionless on the ground, still in her animal form, antlers broken off.

"No, no, no!" The sharp scratch of a talon nicks my arm, and a baby wails, but it doesn't sound like AnnaGrey's cry. Feathers brush against me, but it's so bright that everything in my field of vision is only outlines.

Greyson pulls me away into the light, and we fall, landing in darkness.

FORTY

reyson has taken AnnaGrey from me because I can't control my screaming and crying. I remain on the ground, searching for a way back into the light. Because wherever that is, Faylia is there, and so is a dying aeobanach who risked her life to save us. Whose filly, Iris, is waiting for a mother who will never come home. But there is nothing but darkness and strange noises. Lights shine in the distance, but none like I've ever seen. AnnaGrey cries, and Greyson coos and rocks her, but she continues to wail. I drag myself off the ground and scream at the trees, the ones that bow to each other, the ones that ignore me and refuse to light again. The familiar sound of heavy wings beats against the air, and I seek the sky, waiting to see a crowe or a paison. There is a flash of red, then nothing.

"Saffron!" I yell. "Saffron, you coward!"

"Anna," Greyson says, but I ignore him because AnnaGrey is crying, and we're lost, and the light that was once blinding has left us in darkness.

"Faylia," I cry, "Faylia!" I sink to my knees. "What happened? Where are we?"

"I don't think we're in the realm anymore."

"What in the blackest holes are you talking about?" I snap.

"The Gates."

"Gates?" Something dings in my brain, reminding me of something Phoenix had said. The Morgate... or was it Mergate? Or Norgate? I look at Greyson. "The Morgate? Mergate?"

"I don't know. I've only heard rumors, whispers. I think it's called the Mergate. It's supposed to be near the sea."

"Well. If it's a gate, we have to figure out how to get through it."

Greyson looks down at his now-sleeping daughter. "There must be magic of some kind."

I throw up my arms in despair. "Then, let's find it."

"She needs milk," Greyson says, handing AnnaGrey to me. "Hide. I'll be back."

AnnaGrey and I curl up near the trees. I glare at them, silently trying to get them to give up their secrets. The premonition I'd had that I wouldn't see Faylia again slams into my mind as if it's telling me, "I told you so." My best friend, the only one who stayed by my side. The thought nearly sends me into hysterics again.

I curse the universe. I don't need to hide. I don't need to cower anymore. Everyone I love is safe from Saffron, so why am I now locked away from them? What is this place, and why are we in it? I grasp the roots of my hair, and I pull out a black feather that is tangled in it. With a grunt of disgust, I toss the wretched thing away from me. It has to be Saffron's. My hair got caught up in his plumage when he crashed into me.

But then I remember he has my ring, and that he painted it with my blood.

I crawl to where the feather landed and clench it in my hands. A small pinprick of his blood has dried at the root where it was yanked from his body.

Now I have my enemy's blood, too.

Hours later, Greyson returns. The bottle he hands me is

strange, and the milk is cold, but AnnaGrey drinks it down. He doesn't say a word, just stares in the distance.

Finally, I say, "Where are we?"

His eyes are unfocused when he speaks. "I don't know."

"Where did you get the milk?"

"I… don't know."

"Greyson!"

He shakes himself and looks at me.

"Did you forget I was here?"

"Anna…." He trails off. "We can't survive here."

"We'll just have to find a way until we can get home."

"This is like no place I have ever been."

"I can hide us."

Greyson swallows hard. His throat moves, and he opens his mouth as if he's trying to say something. He shakes his head, then says, "I don't know how to get us home. If those trees are a gateway, then we are in a different world."

I wouldn't have believed him had I not heard Phoenix and Helaine discussing another gate. I would say it's unreal, but the evidence slaps me in the face. Strange lights, strange sounds, strange milk to give to AnnaGrey.

Where are we, and how do we get home?

We say little else. We fall asleep and wake to a beautiful wood, but it isn't our wood in our realm. These woods are wild, tangled brambles and brush crawling over it with no broken paths.

I strangle the trees, begging them to open. Greyson gets more milk and brings us strange bread and odd fruit. He tells me about this place we're in, that the creatures here don't appear to have animal forms, only human forms.

I have lost everything. Again. Even my place. And I blame Greyson. He pulled me into the light. I bury my face in my hands and concentrate on breathing because that's the only thing I have control of, even if it's coming in deep, uneven gasps. The light in the wood is softer when I look up, as if I've been sitting this way for hours. Maybe I have been. I don't know. AnnaGrey cries, and I figure she must need a wrap change. She is the only thing that makes me move rather than lie down in front of the trees that form the gate.

I square my shoulders and stand.

"Fine," I say, breaking the silence in the wood. "If this is to be my new home, then so be it."

Greyson blinks, apparently unaware that I've come back to the living. He's fumbling with the fur wrap that holds AnnaGrey.

I take her from him, disentangling her little body. "I need clean wrappings."

He digs into a satchel that he's carrying and hands it to me. I busy myself with cleaning her off, with looking into her crescent eyes that blink up at me. I secure her in furs and stand, then sway from side to side, rocking her to sleep. She yawns and smacks her rosebud lips. I make a vow to myself. She must survive because she doesn't deserve any of this.

"Anna, the realm—"

But whatever he was going to say is lost with my final snarl. "Do not speak of the realm to me again. If we are stranded here, so be it. I have lost more than just my home before."

AnnaGrey makes a cooing sound. I swaddle her tighter and hand her to her father, and then make my way to the treeline in the distance. Perhaps being locked out of the realm is the best thing because Saffron will never find us here, and I won't have to use my invisibility every day to shield AnnaGrey. She can live, have a full life. I can live without fear. I can be seen.

London will never know what happened to us, but at least Saffron can no longer use us against her. She will be free to reign over Miadien and keep it safe. It's what she always wanted. There's nothing I can do about it, anyway. We are locked out.

I glance over my shoulder. Greyson has come up behind me, AnnaGrey in his arms. The trees that formed the gate sway slightly, as if bidding us goodbye.

I will not think of them again.

Lindsay Flanagan writes fantasy stories to empower girls to embrace their unique traits and weave their own spells into the world. Her debut novel, *AnnaGrey and the Constellation,* is the first runner-up in the middle reader category of the Eric Hoffer Book Award and a First Horizon Medal Finalist for 2024. The middle grade fantasy is what Book Viral Reviews calls "reminiscent of some of the great fantasies of this era."

She is also the author of *The Forsaken,* a collection of poetry, short stories, creative prose, and photography, written and photographed over the span of twenty years.

When she's not writing, she's editing other authors' stories or teaching about writing. She lives in Utah with her husband, two daughters, three dogs, and sometimes a horse.

www.ingramcontent.com/pod-product-compliance
Lightning Source LLC
Chambersburg PA
CBHW022139240626
47153CB00007B/2415